F
Lehrer

Lehrer, James.

Eureka.

DATE			

EUREKA

EUREKA

A NOVEL

Jim Lehrer

RANDOM HOUSE / NEW YORK

Published in the United States by Random House, an imprint
of The Random House Publishing Group, a division of Random
House, Inc., New York.

RANDOM HOUSE and colophon are registered trademarks
of Random House, Inc.

Permissions acknowledgments can be found on page 229.

LIBRARY OF CONGRESS CATALOGING-IN-PUBLICATION DATA
Lehrer, James.
Eureka: a novel / Jim Lehrer.
p.   cm.
ISBN 978-1-4000-6487-8
1. Insurance agents—Fiction. 2. Midlife crisis—Fiction.
3. Self-actualization (Psychology)—Fiction. 4. Kansas—Fiction.
5. Psychological fiction. I. Title.
PS3562.E4419E97 2007   813'.54—dc22   2006051884

Printed in the United States of America on acid-free paper

www.atrandom.com

9 8 7 6 5 4 3 2

Fic

To three who won't grow up:
Dave McManaway, Roger Rosenblatt,
and Ben Bradlee

EUREKA

ONE

A TOY FIRE truck set off the series of events that changed the life of Otis Halstead, CEO of Kansas Central Fire and Casualty.

The small cast-iron vehicle was for sale at the Great Prairie Antiques Show at the Marriott Eureka–East on a Saturday afternoon in March. Otis's wife, Sally, had pretty much forced him to attend the show's kickoff luncheon because, as one of the leading businessmen and citizens here in Eureka, Kansas, he should be seen supporting such a good cause—the battered women's shelter run by the Ashland Clinic. Also, their good friend Mary Gidney was the cochair of the whole thing.

Sally then insisted that Otis go with her on a quick walk through the show in the hotel's large exhibition hall. "Why not at least take a look at what is being offered for sale?" she said. More than five hundred antiques dealers from more than thirty states had set up.

"That's it!" Otis shouted. "I found it!"

He aimed an index finger at something in the stall of a dealer from Connecticut. He seemed to be pointing toward an expensive Chippendale dining room chest.

"That cabinet doesn't fit with our decor, and it's probably a fortune anyhow," Sally said. "What's the matter with you, Otis? Lower your voice."

"The fire engine, not the cabinet," he said. "That red one with the white rubber tires and the firemen sitting in the seats in front and standing on both sides of the rear running boards." The words came rushing out loudly. "I wanted one of those for Christmas when I was five years old. I wanted it so badly it gave me diarrhea."

"All right, now. People are beginning to stare," said Sally. "You're no longer five, Otis."

"I still believed in Santa Claus and had written him a note at the North Pole about it. I went to the live Santa at Buck's in Wichita and every other place I could find one."

He moved a step closer to the truck. Sally grabbed his right arm and held it tight. Here they were, a well-dressed couple of substance—he in a blue blazer and matching outfit, she in a light pink suit ensemble. They stood fast, rigidly facing a ten-inch toy in a cabinet under five feet away.

"Everybody knew I wanted that fire engine and *only* that fire engine. But I didn't get it. I raced out to see what was under the tree, and that fire engine wasn't there."

"Time to go on home now, Otis my darling. I really do appreciate your coming with me today—giving up your Saturday afternoon." She looked into his face. "Are those tears? Please, now. This is so unlike you."

Otis, still staring at the toy, said, "I cried and pouted the rest of Christmas Day and for weeks afterward. Mom said Santa must have run out of those fire engines before he got to our house. Dad said Santa must have decided it was too expensive or too heavy to cart all the way to Kansas from the North Pole. It cost fourteen dollars and weighed a pound and a half at the most."

Sally released her grip on his arm and raised her hands in an act of surrender. "I can't believe this is happening."

They went over to the cabinet together. Otis picked up the toy. The two miniature firemen on the front seat and the two on the back and four on the sides were looking straight ahead with their painted eyes. All were wearing firemen's helmets and coats and boots that had been stamped onto them.

A young salesman, tweedy and eager, joined Otis and Sally. "Mint condition, all the way," he said. "No restoration—everything on it is original, even the paint."

So was the price, inked in small numbers on a white tag hanging around the fireman driver's neck: $12,350.

Sally was stunned. "For a toy?"

"Antique toys like this—this was made by the Arcade Company, one of the finest cast-iron toy manufacturers in history —are going for astronomical prices these days," said the young man. He extended his hands about two and a half feet apart and added, "We sold a cast-iron Pickwick Nite Coach sleeper bus— early-thirties vintage—about this size last month for twenty-two thousand, if you can believe it."

Sally said she preferred not to believe it.

Otis said, "Do you take American Express?"

"Otis!" Sally exclaimed. "Twelve thousand dollars for a toy?"

He said, "It's mine. It just took fifty-four years for Santa to make delivery."

THEIR BRAND-NEW blue 1997 BMW was considered Sally's car, but Otis drove it to their home in NorthPark, Eureka's most exclusive, upscale, and expensive neighborhood. Otis always did the driving when they were together. It was one of the many standard practices in their thirty-seven years of life together that buying expensive antique toys on a whim did not fit.

It especially didn't fit Otis, who, at age fifty-nine, was mostly a medium: medium height, weight, build, and temperament. The only radical thing about him was the top of his head, which was bald.

Once in their house, Otis, without taking off his jacket or saying a word, put the fire engine down on the polished dark walnut floor in the den. Soon he was on his hands and knees, scooting it between the legs of chairs, over throw rugs, through twists of electric cords, up against desks, bookcases, and wastebaskets.

"Please don't make the sound of a siren or a motor," said Sally.

Otis heard her but didn't respond, either with words or with any other sounds. He was busy concentrating on whipping the toy truck around a hard turn at a mahogany magazine stand.

"Well, at least you're showing some interest in something besides Kansas Central Fire and Casualty," Sally said as she left Otis to play by himself. "I'm looking for a bright side."

Next came the BB gun.

IT WAS AN official Daisy Red Ryder air rifle. Otis ordered it for $39.95 from a Nostalgia Today catalog because it was exactly like the one he'd wanted with all of his heart and soul when he was ten years old. His mother had said no way in hell or Kansas, because those things were too dangerous and he would put out his own or somebody else's eye with a BB. His father said BB guns were for rich people anyhow and much too expensive for you and us, Otis. Same as cast-iron fire trucks.

But now Otis Halstead didn't have to pay attention to what his parents said, because, among other things, they were both dead. That left mostly Sally to do the talking.

"At least it doesn't cost a fortune, like that fire engine, Otis," she said.

"You're moving toward a second childhood, Otis," she said.

"Grow back up, Otis," she said.

"I'm delighted you're enjoying yourself away from the office, but this is getting a bit strange, Otis," she said.

Otis loved his BB gun from the second he took it out of the box and held it in his hands. Three or four guys in his high school had had them, and holding theirs nearly fifty years ago was the last and only time he had done so.

Now, finally, on an early Wednesday evening after a hard day as CEO of an insurance company, he had his very own.

It was thirty-six inches of wood and metal and shooting perfection that weighed just over two pounds. The dark wood stock was engraved with a drawing of Red Ryder, the famous redheaded cowboy of the comics and movies, tossing a lasso from his horse. The rope was configured in the air to spell RED RYDER. On top of the black metal barrel were two stationary sights eighteen inches apart. Hanging from the right near the trigger was a foot-long leather lanyard, designed for carrying the gun on a cowboy's saddle just like Red Ryder did his rifle.

There was also a supply of BBs. They were in a separate orange cardboard box that was the size and style of a coffee-cream carton. Printed on top was RED RYDER JR. TREASURE CHEST. On the sides was Red Ryder on his horse, running along with his Indian boy sidekick and friend, Little Beaver. Inside were twenty-three cellophane Quick Silver packs of BBs—150 in a pack—plus several paper targets and some historical information on Red Ryder. There was also an invitation to visit a museum in Pagosa Springs, Colorado, where the original comic book drawings of Red Ryder were on display.

There were also booklets on general air rifle safety and the care and use of the Daisy air rifle. There were instructions on everything from how to load the BBs—through a hole along the right side of the barrel—to suggestions for games of marksman skill that could be played, including tic-tac-toe.

Otis immediately loaded the rifle and invited Sally to join him in the backyard for an inaugural game of BB tic-tac-toe. She declined.

So he went by himself to what their architect and builder had described as an outside entertainment area. All it was to Otis was a very large—fifty by forty feet—and very expensive gray slate patio with year-round garden furniture, a built-in gas grill, and a stereo system that played CDs as well as tapes. Beyond the patio was a patch of golf-green lawn for croquet or volleyball and a forty-foot-long swimming pool. The whole area was lit by an elaborate but discreet system of lights hung at various levels from several tall trees—mostly cottonwoods and sycamores— that encircled the entire area.

Instead of making a tic-tac-toe board, Otis grabbed one of the printed targets, a ten-inch-square piece of heavy off-white paper with five black half-inch-wide rings going out from a solid bull's-eye. It was a standard shooters' target, with each ring carrying a certain number of points—fifty for hitting the bull's-eye, ten for the outermost ring.

Otis fastened one of the paper targets on a tree with a thumbtack, moved back to a position ten yards away, cocked the BB gun with its pump lever, sighted the bull's-eye, and squeezed off a BB.

It missed the target—and the tree.

The next shot struck the paper, at least, but not within any of the rings. He kept shooting until it was almost dark, and by the time he finished, he was hitting a bull's-eye at least every tenth or eleventh shot.

It confirmed what he had suspected from his childhood in Sedgwicktown—he was a natural-born BB gun marksman, a natural-born Red Ryder.

He was back out there in the morning before breakfast and shot off another twenty BBs.

He did the same thing the next morning and the next and the next, reporting his scores to Sally. "Four bull's-eyes, three fifties, five twenty-fives, and only six that were tens or out of the money. Does it make you proud?"

It was on his tenth straight morning of shooting that Sally said, "I talked to Mary Gidney about your problem. She says there's a man out at Ashland Clinic who specializes in treating what you're doing. She said she'd ask Bob."

The Ashland Clinic—the world-famous Ashland Clinic, as it was called around Eureka—was one of the most prominent small mental health institutions in the country. Its prominence in Eureka made the open discussion of mental health problems, psychotherapy, and psychoanalysis as routine around town as steaks in Kansas City, Fords in Detroit, and movies in Hollywood. Mary Gidney's husband, Bob, was the clinic's top authority on paranoid schizophrenia.

"You mean there's a guy at Ashland who treats only grown men who buy toy fire engines and Daisy Red Ryder air rifles?" said Otis, who may have been one of a handful of Eurekans over the age of fourteen who hadn't had at least one session with some kind of Ashland professional.

"Mary said there's probaby even a name for what you have, but she couldn't place what it was. Some kind of syndrome or 'ism' or 'philia.' "

"BB-ism? Fire-truck-ism? Air-rifle-philia?"

"I'm serious, Otis. It has to do with men turning back into children," Sally said, waving him away as if he were a problem child. "There was a play, and a movie, in the seventies about some New Mexico weirdos, and one of them thought he was Red Ryder. It was called *When You Comin' Back, Red Ryder?* I believe."

"And they've got someone at the world-famous Ashland Clinic who treats *Kansas* weirdos with Red-Ryder-itis?"

Again, Sally waved him off.

Otis ignored her Ashland suggestion and kept up his daily shooting. What he quit doing was reporting his daily scores to Sally.

Within two more weeks, he was up to hitting bull's-eyes at least ten out of every twenty shots. It made him wonder if there were competition shoots for the BB gun. Think of the trophies, the glory, the fame—the T-shirts, the pennants, the embroidered patches, the autographed photos.

He laughed out loud at the prospect of telling Sally he was going to be gone for a weekend competing in the official Daisy Red Ryder Air Rifle Championship in someplace like Pagosa Springs, Colorado.

OTIS GIRARD HALSTEAD of Sedgwicktown and Sally Jewell Winfield of Independence had met thirty-nine years earlier while students at the University of Kansas at Lawrence. She had come to KU to get a degree in drama and left with one in English. He had come with no plans other than to graduate and left with a degree in business administration.

Sally's drama interest came with her from Independence, which was the hometown of William Inge, the playwright who won awards and fame for his straightforward plays—*Come Back, Little Sheba, Bus Stop, Picnic, The Dark at the Top of the Stairs,* among others—about the ordinary people of small-town America. Sally's parents ran Winfield's, a small dry-goods store on Main Street that Sally's grandfather had started in the late 1800s. The Inge influence permeated the whole town, particularly the schools, which sent more than one kid out into the world wanting to be a playwright or novelist, director, actor, or actress.

Sally Winfield's Inge thing had been acting. Her dream had been to portray the lead females in all of William Inge's plays on any and every stage in America and the world.

She and Otis met while she was playing such a role. He was in the student infirmary at KU, recuperating from a broken ankle; she was there with a group of drama students to provide entertainment for the student patients as part of a class project.

Otis was in pain, unable to walk, and certain his life was in ruin when this beautiful blond creature came into the ward. She and a crew-cut guy from Wichita wearing cowboy boots did a scene from near the end of *Bus Stop.* She played Cherie, who was being asked by a young man named Bo to come away and marry him.

"Cherie . . . it's awful hard for a fella, after he's been turned down once, to git up enough guts to try again."

"Ya don't need guts, Bo."

"I don't?"

"It's the last thing in the world ya need."

"Well . . . Anyway, I just don't have none now, so I'll just have to say what I feel in my heart."

"Yeah?"

"I still wish you was goin' back to the ranch with me, more 'n anything I know."

"Ya do?"

"Yeah, I do."

"Why, I'd go anywhere in the world with ya now, Bo. Anywhere at all."

"Ya would? Ya would?"

Otis decided there and then that once he got back on his feet and out of this place, he was going to find that blond student actress and do everything in his power to persuade her to go to *his* ranch or wherever with him.

He found her three years later. Otis had to first find a job before taking on a wife and family. They stayed in touch and saw each other often, but Sally spent the time working in her parents' store in Independence. Her life with Otis, when it did begin, was one that had no stage appearances in any William Inge play, or any other, for that matter. Sally's drama professor at KU—a retired stage character actor named Overbrook—had preached the message that acting was a life, not a hobby. So she put it completely aside, to be first a wife, and then a mother— delayed for an additional four years after marriage until Otis could see a solid long-term future at Kansas Central Fire and Casualty—and a good citizen of Eureka, Kansas.

Sally and Otis had had only one real conversation about her stage career that never was. They were driving alone together on the interstate back to Eureka from Kansas City, after seeing Inge's *The Dark at the Top of the Stairs,* which had originally starred Pat Hingle and Teresa Wright, at the Lyric Theatre. Otis and Sally were in their mid-forties, but he had been struck on this particular evening by how young and beautiful Sally still looked. Her bright blond hair, which she wore straight and shoulder-length, shone like an exquisite silk crown, her soft brown eyes were like jewels in that crown, her complexion was like the tan coating on a piece of elegant enameled china . . .

"You could have been as good—and as famous—an actress as Teresa Wright, if you had chosen that instead of me," Otis said.

"We'll never know, will we?" Sally replied.

At first Otis thought he detected a tone of anger and remorse, longing and disappointment, but then she said, "And that's probably just as well, Otis. I never found out for sure, so I will always have my what-if dream instead of disappointment."

A few miles farther down the highway, Otis asked, "If you had known I was going to be bald, would you have given me even a second look, much less given up your acting dream for me?"

Sally reached over with her left hand and caressed the top of his hairless head. But she said not a word.

THE NEXT THING Otis bought was a football helmet.

It was an official regulation NFL helmet of the Kansas City Chiefs, the favorite team of Otis and nearly everyone else in the Eureka area. Kansas City, only forty miles beyond Lawrence and 125 from Eureka, was the big city in the lives of most people in Eureka, even if the largest of the two separate Kansas Cities was on the Missouri rather than the Kansas side of the line.

Otis saw the helmet in the window of a Sports World super-store at the North Side mall, where he had gone Saturday morning to buy a new book about the naval battles of World War II. The helmet's plastic shell was glowing red, with the Chiefs' arrowhead symbol on each side. Without a second's thought, Otis bought it for $185 and went right home to put it on his bald head.

He looked at himself in the mirror over the sink in the downstairs bathroom and very much loved the boy from Sedgwicktown who stared back at him. It was a sight he'd never seen when he was such a boy, and that was what had prompted his impulse decision to buy the helmet.

Otis and all thirty-six of the other boys in Sedgwicktown High School had played on the football team because they'd had no choice. If they hadn't, they would have been labeled "fruits,"

and their lives would have been ruined for high school if not forever, at least in Sedgwicktown. Some played varsity in the games
against Valley Center, Lehigh, Maize, Mount Hope, Haven,
Hesston, and other neighboring Kansas towns. Then there were
the scrubs who scrimmaged only in practice as fodder for the
varsity. Otis was a scrub, too small for a lineman, too slow for a
running back or split end, and too uncoordinated for a quarterback. So he spent every fall afternoon through four years of high
school being tackled, blocked, hammered, slammed, kneed,
elbowed, and thrown around as a live practice dummy.

The worst part was that he didn't even sit on the bench during the games. He was in the stands with the girls because the
Sedgwicktown Cardinals could afford only twenty-five game
helmets. They were shiny white plastic, much like those the college teams then used, with a bright red cardinal on either side.

"Buy your own helmet, and you can suit up," said the coach
to Otis and the other scrubs who didn't—and never would—
make the game cut.

His mother said she was just as happy that Otis wasn't out
there on the football field endangering his life, ignoring the
obvious fact that the coach never would have sent Otis onto the
field. His only endangerment would have been from tripping
over a bucket or getting a splinter in his butt from the wooden
bench.

His dad said wasting money on a football helmet was out of
the question.

"Well, what do you think?" Otis now asked Sally as he walked
into the den with his new Kansas City Chiefs helmet on his
head.

"I think you must get help, Otis," she replied. "You really
must."

"You can't tell I'm bald, can you?" he asked.

"Otis, you're close to being in real trouble."

Otis smiled through the face protector and went outside with his Daisy rifle and shot off some BBs at a target. It was not easy, sighting the rifle with the helmet on, but he soon figured out an effective way to do it.

He fired off ten BBs and then, without really thinking about it, let his aim and the gun rise up and to the right, to a flood-light in one of the trees.

He pulled the trigger. Pow! went the gun. Pop! went the light. Crash! went glass onto the patio.

Within a count of ten, Sally was at the sliding glass door, then outside and inspecting the damage. "You're sick," she said quietly but firmly.

Otis couldn't remember the last time he felt so good.

He spotted a small brown bird on a tree limb off to his left. Again, he aimed and fired a BB. The bird fell from the tree.

"That's it," said Sally.

OTIS KNEW THE "quiet dinner with the Gidneys, just the four of us," was a setup. Sally said it was to have a belated celebration of Mary Gidney's birthday, but that was clearly not so. Otis knew for a fact that Mary had quit celebrating or even acknowledging her birthdays ten years ago. But Otis went along with the line because he really didn't mind talking with Dr. Bob Gidney. Through the years, Otis had known many of the psychiatric types from Ashland Clinic and found them to be about the same ratio of jerks and fools as corporate CEOs or most other lines of work, insurance included. Bob Gidney was a good man, neither a jerk nor a fool. Sally enjoyed being with him as well.

"Hey, that's some fire engine you have there, Otis," said Bob as they came back into the den after dinner. The fire engine was on the mantel over the fireplace. "Something left over from childhood?"

"You might say that," Otis said. He knew what was going on. Sally and Mary, clearly by prearrangement, had lingered in the kitchen. "I just bought it the other day, though."

"That's what I heard," said Bob.

Otis guessed Bob was only a year or two younger, but he always dressed as if he thought he was twenty years younger. Tonight he was in heavy-starched white duck pants, a purple-and-white-checked button-down shirt, and highly polished brown penny loafers with no socks. Otis, who bought most of his clothes from Brooks Brothers and J. Crew catalogs, was wearing khaki chinos, a solid dark blue short-sleeved sport shirt, and white sneakers. Sally often suggested to Otis that he might consider "branching out" and dressing the way Bob Gidney did.

Bob had grown up in the dressy world of Wilmington, Delaware, son of a DuPont executive, and come to Ashland Clinic from Philadelphia, where he taught at the University of Pennsylvania School of Medicine and maintained a private practice.

Otis went over to the fire engine and moved it back and forth across the mantel. "Want to push it around yourself, Bob?"

Bob declined the invitation to play with the fire engine, and in a few moments the two men walked back to the outside entertainment area.

"I hear you bought a BB gun, too?" Bob asked Otis.

"That's right," Otis said, pointing to a cottonwood. "There's my target on that tree. I hit eight straight bull's-eyes this morning—fourteen out of twenty in all."

"Good for you," said Bob.

"You want to fire off a few BBs?" Otis asked. "It's really fun. We can play a game of tic-tac-toe with our shots. It's done the regular way—you can go first. Start in any corner, then—"

Bob shook his head. "I heard about your tic-tac-toe thing."

"Sally clearly gave you a thorough briefing through Mary."

"Sally did it directly," said Bob. "She came to the clinic herself. I had a BB gun when I was fourteen. Got it out of my system. But thanks. And you bought a football helmet? Sally said you wear it around the house a lot. Is that right?"

"It covers my bald head. Want to see it? It's a Chiefs'."

Again, Bob shook his head. "I've seen them on television during the games. Bob Junior has one, too. So do most of his friends." Bob Junior was the Gidneys' thirteen-year-old son.

Otis, ignoring Bob's lack of interest, stepped back inside the house and returned with the Chiefs helmet. He put it on and said, "See? Changes everything about me, doesn't it?"

Bob Gidney said nothing. Otis took off the helmet, turned it over, and showed Bob the inside foam padding and the adjustable headband that held the helmet in place on his head. "I read somewhere that the pros stick things up here in the webbing for good luck during games—money, letters, religious medals, pages from the Bible, condoms, women's panties. Stuff like that."

"I didn't know that, Otis," Bob said.

Otis set the helmet down on a table, and they took seats on the white plastic lawn chairs on the slate patio.

"What's going on, Otis?" Bob asked.

"You're the shrink, you tell me."

"I hate being called a shrink. How would you like being called a bloodsucker—as some people call insurance people?"

What people call us that? thought Otis. But he said, "When you were a kid, you wanted a BB gun, and you got one. Was there anything you really wanted but couldn't have?"

Bob grinned. "My own set of golf clubs. I played on the high school golf team at Wilmington, but always with borrowed clubs. I wanted my own, but there wasn't money to buy them."

"When did you get your own?"

"After medical school. The first time I had more than a few bucks, I bought a set from a friend. I didn't have that much time to play golf, but I wanted the clubs, just in case."

"What else? Maybe something you never did get."

Bob really was no fool. Otis could tell that he knew what all of this was leading to, but he didn't seem to mind.

"A Cushman motor scooter," said Bob.

"Me, too!"

"A red one."

"They only came in red. At least I never saw one in any other color."

"Me, neither. Five or six guys in our school had them. And they always had a gorgeous girl sitting behind them, holding on for dear life. My parents thought motor scooters were too dangerous, too expensive, and too exhibitionist."

"Same, same, same with me. God, what a coincidence. I wonder if they even still make Cushmans."

"Don't even think about it, Otis," Bob said. "Drive up to this house someday with a Cushman, and I promise you, Sally will make me commit you."

"Then why don't *you* buy one, and I can borrow it occasionally?"

"I don't want a motor scooter anymore. I wanted one when I was twelve years old, but I'm not twelve years old anymore."

"Speak for yourself, Bob."

"I just did."

It was time to rejoin the ladies for dessert. Bob got up from his chair, and then Otis did.

"We've got a man at the clinic who is right up your alley, Otis," Bob said. "His name is Russ Tonganoxie. He's new, and he's a bit on the different side. But he's the best in this field."

And what exactly is this field? Otis thought to ask but decided not to, because he really didn't want to hear the answer.

Bob said, "Let me know—or you can have Sally call me—when you want to talk to him."

He made it sound inevitable.

TWO

IS NAME WAS Roger Atchison, but he said most everyone called him "The Cushman King" because he owned more and knew more about Cushman motor scooters than any other human being on the face of the earth.

"Take a deep breath, Mr. Halstead, because you're about to have your breath taken away," Atchison said as he opened the door to a large white warehouse-type metal building in the small Nebraska town of Marion.

Over the door was a three-foot red sign in script that said CUSHMAN HEAVEN. Under it, in smaller letters, were the words "Thou shalt not love thy Cushman more than thy wife and children: as much, but not more."

Otis stepped inside and, yes, immediately had his breath taken away.

"Have you ever seen anything like it?" Atchison asked Otis.

"No, sir," replied Otis.

No, Otis had never seen this many Cushman motor scooters in one place in his life.

"One hundred and thirty-four and still counting," said Atchison. "One hundred and thirty-four and still counting."

Otis had heard him the first time. One hundred and thirty-four Cushman motor scooters. There were 134 Cushman motor scooters out there on a shiny painted light blue concrete floor, assembled in a precise formation of at least ten lines, like soldiers awaiting inspection by a general, a president—or a king.

Roger Atchison didn't look like a king of anything. He was a tall, thin, crew-cut, tanned, smiling, fidgety, chattering man in his mid-sixties who could have passed for a retired Coca-Cola bottler or mayor of Marion, Nebraska, both of which he was. Today he was dressed in blue jeans and a red Windbreaker with CUSHMAN emblazoned in yellow on the back. It was written in the same script style—obviously from the old company logo—that had been used on the sign outside.

Otis had gotten Atchison's name and phone number from a Harley-Davidson dealer in Eureka whom he called in search of information about buying a Cushman motor scooter. He also had sent his secretary down the street to the reference department of the Eureka public library for some basic information on Cushman. So by the time he called Atchison and made an appointment, Otis already knew that Cushman was a Nebraska gasoline motor manufacturing company that had quit making motor scooters in the late 1960s. But there were several thousand of their scooters still out there, most of them restored and cared for as prized treasures from or reminders of their owners' past.

In other words, if Otis needed some Ashland Clinic help, so did a lot of other people.

Most particularly, this man Roger Atchison. He had been talking about Cushmans almost nonstop from the moment Otis pulled his Ford Explorer up to the front door of Atchison's home, two blocks down the street from Cushman Heaven.

Now, inside heaven itself, Atchison's voice, nasal and excited, was the only sound.

"I've got 'em lined up in chronological order. The first is a 1938 Auto-Glide, the last's a 1965 Eagle, one of the last scooters Cushman ever made. The factory was just forty miles up the road from here in Lincoln. Lincoln's our capital and where our university is, too. Go, you Huskers. The Auto-Glide's a traditional step-through, the Eagle's a straddle."

Oh, yes, thought Otis. The straddle style meant a rider sat down with his legs on either side of the scooter, as if it were a horse or a regular motorcycle. On the step-through, the rider sat with his legs in front, on a cushioned seat over the small motor, as on a chair. The scooters Otis had longed for in Sedgwicktown, Kansas, forty years ago were all step-throughs. Those late '40s–early '50s models were the only kind he knew or cared about.

But he followed Atchison over to the red 1938 Auto-Glide to begin the troop through the entire formation.

"This was the Deluxe Auto-Glide, a little jewel with a storage battery, large headlamps, a taillight, an electric horn, and a lock for the ignition and lights—the whole nine yards. It's got a one-and-a-half-horsepower engine, hard to start. Mostly had to hope you had a hill to coast down to get it to fire up. A Cushman dealer paid about a hundred dollars apiece for this baby and then sold them retail for one-fifty or so. Red and blue were the main colors of Cushmans. Then they came in with a green. The paint was the same kind used on tractors and other farm vehicles . . ."

Chatter, chatter up and down the lines, stopping for an occasional detailed description of the machine and its various parts and characteristics.

Otis soon spotted his—the one he wanted. It was a red 1952 Pacemaker, exactly like the one that drove him crazy with envy during his high school years. Jackson Hays got one and, with it, stole the woman Otis loved. She was a blond knockout named Julie Ann—he could no longer remember her last name: Wakeeney? Wakefield? Wallace? After going steady with Otis for two years, she dropped him for Jackson and his motor scooter. Otis could still see the bitch sitting up there behind Jackson, her breasts and other warm frontal body parts hard up against Jackson's excited back and her arms tight around his waist.

Roger Atchison, the Cushman King, described this Pacemaker. "Traditional step-through 'chair' style, as you can see. Single speed, automatic clutch drive, Cushman 100 tires, good lights. Great seat there on the back for a lovely lady. Storage compartment down there behind it that'll hold the groceries and a lot more. Sold retail for about two-ninety-five—two hundred to the dealers. Among the best of the best."

Otis began the courtship. "How much would one of these cost now? If you could find one like this one, say, that was for sale."

"Oh, well," said The Cushman King, "they are really hard to come by, and that is what makes them expensive—supply and demand, you know."

Otis knew. "So, ballpark price?"

"Depending on the condition, anywhere from thirty-five hundred to five thousand."

"How about one like yours here, one that's in perfect condition?"

"Oh, it would bring five, no problem. But it's not for sale. I seldom sell any of mine."

Otis knew what was going on, and Roger Atchison clearly knew Otis knew he knew. But that was part of the fun, the game—the courting.

Otis said, "When you do sell one, what does it take?"

"Oh, that's hard to say. This is the only red 1952 Pacemaker

I have, and I haven't even thought about what it would be like to live without it in particular, or with only one hundred and thirty-three scooters and still counting instead of one hundred and thirty-four. I only part with a scooter that I feel I can live without or is a duplicate or the offer is just so high no reasonable person could turn it down."

Otis asked if $7,500 fell into the last category.

"It does indeed, sir," said Atchison, extending his right hand. "Congratulations on taking your first step toward creating your own little piece of Cushman Heaven."

They rolled the Pacemaker out of line and outside into a large parking lot, where Atchison gave Otis a few minutes' instruction on how to start and operate the scooter.

Otis was startled by the joy and by the tingles and tremors of excitement that rushed through his body as he tooled that scooter around.

Look at me now, Julie Ann whatever-your-last-name-was!

The viability of Otis's personal check for $7,500 was verified by phone with the First National Bank of Eureka, the one-way rental of a small trailer from Ryder was arranged, and soon Otis Halstead departed Roger Atchison's Cushman Heaven with a red 1952 Pacemaker.

Otis also left wearing a two-and-a-half-inch round button that said, I ♥ MY CUSHMAN.

"I promise you, Mr. Halstead, that your life will never be the same again," Atchison had said as he pinned the button to Otis's shirtfront during a brief departure ceremony.

OTIS DROVE THE Explorer, the Cushman-bearing trailer behind it, into the semicircular driveway in front of his house.

Out the front door poured a group of mostly upset people.

Sally was there, as was Annabel, their KU graduate school daughter. So were the Gidneys and Pete Wetmore, the executive vice president of Kansas Central Fire and Casualty, plus two plainclothes detectives from the Eureka police department.

Sally had been crying. "We thought you might be dead," she said.

"Or kidnapped for ransom, or raped," said Annabel, who was dry-eyed.

"Raped?" Sally gasped aloud. "We're talking about your father. Men don't get raped, for God's sake. They do the raping."

"Things have changed out there in the world, Mom," replied Annabel.

"Not in the world of Kansas, they haven't!" Sally responded angrily.

Amen! Otis wanted to shout.

"We were also concerned about a possible hostage situation," said Pete. He had been hired to be the heir apparent of the company, a step Otis had come to regret. He found Pete, who was only forty-two, a dreary man with the soul of a seventy-year-old who seldom risked anything, laughed, or even smiled.

"We were about to notify the FBI," said the older of the two detectives, who was gray, overweight, and seemed tired and bored with all of this crap among these rich people. "They'd have probably put a tap on the phone in case a ransom—or death—call came in."

Only Bob Gidney seemed to notice the 1952 Pacemaker on the trailer. "You did it," he said to Otis. "You did it."

Otis thought he had planned his trip to Nebraska in a way that he would not be missed until he was back in Eureka with a Cushman. He had told his office that he was going to spend the day at home, getting caught up on some material for a speech he had to make at the company's annual meeting in two weeks. He had told Sally he would be away from the office all day, working on some figures for the upcoming annual meeting. He had driven off toward Marion shortly before seven-thirty that morning in the Explorer, feeling pretty good about his arrangements. He had correctly estimated under eight hours for the trip up and back, including viewing and negotiating time. It was now three in the afternoon, and the whole thing might have worked if Annabel hadn't suddenly decided to come home to spend the day trying to get over a fight she'd had with her latest boyfriend. She had left Lawrence in such a hurry that she'd forgotten her key to the house in Eureka, and when she found Sally not at home, she drove to Otis's office. His secretary's search for her missing boss eventually led to a series of phone calls, and before long the word was out that Otis had disappeared. The fear of a crime had been raised.

That fear, Otis knew, was generated by the fact that he had never ever—maybe in his whole life—done anything so irresponsible. Never ever—maybe in his whole life—had he ever simply disappeared for a few hours without telling Sally or his secretary or his mother or his teacher or somebody.

Otis the Responsible, that's me.

He apologized to everyone for the inconvenience and anxiety his disappearance had caused. Otis had been so certain he would get away with being gone a few hours that he had not worked on any contrite remarks. "I really am sorry, I really am" was all he said.

"How about some help getting this scooter off the trailer?" he said after he tired of saying he was sorry.

The older detective, Jerry Elkhart, and Bob Gidney walked out to the trailer.

"I had a Cushman Road King when I was growing up," said the detective. He spoke with animation, as if he was alive after all. "Wasn't it the next one up the line from the Pacemaker?"

"You know your Cushmans. That's right," said Otis. He had seen at least five Road Kings in Cushman Heaven and recalled that Atchison had said the main difference was the transmission. The Pacemaker operated in only one gear, while the Road King had two. There were also some cosmetic differences—better lights and more chrome trimming, for example.

"Did you just buy this thing?" the detective asked.

Otis said he had indeed.

"How much did it set you back, if you don't mind my asking?"

"A couple of thousand or so," Otis lied. He was not about to tell this policeman or anyone else that he paid $7,500 for the old scooter.

"Mine cost two hundred and fifty-seven dollars in 1954. I remember that exactly because my dad loaned me the money, and it took me three years on a paper route and bagging groceries to pay him back."

The scooter had been secured to the trailer with large leather straps. Detective Elkhart and Dr. Gidney helped Otis roll and lift the red scooter down and onto the driveway.

Otis immediately sat down on the scooter's seat, hit the kick starter with his right foot, gunned it with the throttle on the right handlebar, released the brake with his left foot, and smoothly moved off. He did four big U-turns out into the street—there was no traffic—and came back.

"Want to give it a twirl for old times' sake?" he asked Elkhart.

It had been a while since Otis had seen such a wide and glorious smile on another man's face. Elkhart, proving that you never forget how to ride a motor scooter as well as a bicycle, took possession and control and rode off as if he did it every day.

When he returned after two long spins down the street and back, Otis asked Bob Gidney if he'd like a turn.

Bob smiled, mounted the Pacemaker, and rode off down the street.

It was only then that Otis thought to look back at the front of the house to see what the rest of his welcoming committee might be doing. Dreary Pete Wetmore was still standing there, looking stunned. The other detective, who appeared to be about twenty-five, was talking on his cellphone.

Sally was no longer there. But Annabel was. Her face was frozen in a look of absolute amazement.

IT WAS A lovely, quiet, dreamy Sunday afternoon on the soft grassy bank of Farnsworth Creek. The daffodils, petunias, and sunflowers smelled sweet and shone brightly under the April Kansas sun. The temperature was in the comfortable low eighties, the breezes were gentle and fluffy.

Under a majestic cottonwood tree lay an exquisitely tanned beautiful young woman on a flowery quilt, reading a book, *Taking Charge* by Michael Beschloss. She was dressed in pleated yellow shorts and a pastel blue short-sleeved blouse. Her long blond hair lay above her head on a small pillow.

Into this tranquil scene came the soft putt-putt of a small gasoline motor. From down a narrow gravel path emerged a red 1952 Cushman Pacemaker ridden by a man wearing a red Kansas City Chiefs football helmet, with a Daisy Red Ryder BB gun strapped to the right side.

The woman, who appeared to be in her mid-twenties, sat up at the intrusion and watched in clear fear as the armed man and the scooter came to a halt under ten yards away.

Otis Halstead waved to her and turned off the motor. "Sorry to bother you," he said as he leaned forward from his seat and put both feet on the ground.

The woman said nothing, did nothing.

"You should listen to the tapes, too," said Otis after noticing her book, which she had set down on the quilt beside her. "Hearing Lyndon Johnson's voice saying all of that is truly a most special experience."

The Beschloss book and accompanying tapes from Lyndon Johnson's first months as president after the assassination of John F. Kennedy had been one of Sally's Christmas presents to Otis last year. He enjoyed reading contemporary American history.

Otis stepped off the scooter on the left side and whacked down the kickstand with his right foot.

The young woman, sitting with her arms across her bent legs, remained perfectly still and silent.

Otis removed the BB gun from the scooter and held it sideways toward the woman. "It's a Daisy Red Ryder air rifle," he said. "It's a kid's toy, bought it out of a catalog."

The muscles in her face seemed to loosen a bit. The expression of fear and concern was replaced by one of interest and curiosity. But she said nothing. The only sounds were the water flowing in the creek and the rustle of leaves in the cottonwood tree.

Otis leaned the gun against the side of the scooter and walked toward the water, away from the woman. Without looking at her, he said, "On days like this, it makes you wonder why Dorothy or Judy Garland ever wanted to leave Kansas, doesn't it?"

"I've never wanted to leave Kansas," the young woman said. Her voice was as soft and gentle as the breezes. Or that's the way it sounded to Otis, who turned back to face her. She was smiling.

"You must be, as the old song said, a real 'sunflower from the Sunflower State,' " he said.

"What song is that?" she said. "I know about 'Home on the Range.' Is there another one about Kansas?"

He wanted to say: Yes, yes. "Sunflower" by Mack David. Russ Morgan's recording of it had made the 1949 *Hit Parade* on the radio. And he wanted to sing it for her. He knew the words to all four verses and the refrain. There had been a time long ago when Otis knew the words to hundreds of popular songs.

But he did not sing "Sunflower" for this young woman. Instead, he said, "Have you come to the part in the book where LBJ talks about Bobby Kennedy?"

"No, not yet. I don't think I've ever seen a scooter like that before."

"It's an antique."

"Why not just buy a new one?"

Otis decided there was no answer to that question that he wanted to give the young woman. He turned back toward the creek, which was clear and about fifty yards wide at this particular spot in the Cimarron Regional Park. Otis had been coming here for years to fish and to walk.

This was the first time he had come on a Cushman and the first time he had come across a beautiful young woman reading a book.

"Why haven't you taken off the football helmet?" she asked.

"My head will come off with it if I do," Otis replied, turning back to face her.

She laughed. "What's your name?" she asked.

Without a second's hesitation, Otis said, "Buck."

Buck? Buck. There had been a guy from Sedgwicktown who played starting halfback for K-State when Otis was a freshman in high school. His name was Buck—Buck Kingman. He came back to town occasionally and walked the streets surrounded by squads of admiring boys and girls. Otis had always thought it would be terrific to be named Buck. Now he was.

"What's your name?" Otis asked the girl.

"Sharon."

"What brings you here?"

"Well, it's so lovely and peaceful. I just moved to Eureka from Wichita—I'm a nurse. And you?"

"I'm not allowed to talk about myself," he said. "Would you like to take a ride on my scooter? I'm a good driver—and safe in every respect."

Without a word, she stood up.

He hung the air rifle by its lanyard on the handlebars, kick-started the motor, and she climbed up behind him.

And then he felt the thrill, the glory, the incredible turn-on of her hands lightly on his waist and the warmth of her body against his back as they rode away together down the gravel path.

What if Annabel is right? And this young thing decides to rape me?

THEY RODE DOWN the path a hundred yards or so onto a little-used connecting blacktop road and then circled back to the creek bank. They neither passed nor saw nor heard any other vehicles or people.

For Otis, it was twenty minutes of being in a high, unrelenting state of exquisite sexual arousal unlike anything he had experienced in a long time—so long that he couldn't even recall the last time he had felt anything quite like it.

He could feel her young breath on his neck, her young fingers in his belt loops, and on a few delicious occasions when the scooter turned or lurched, he felt some of the most intimate parts of her young body pressed against his back.

She must be about half his own age, younger even than Annabel. Otis, a Dole-Kassebaum Republican, thought of Bill

Clinton, the Arkansas fool, fouling his presidency and place in history over a girl like this.

Otis the Responsible wasn't about to lose anything over sex, but thoughts of Clinton's fate did not, at that moment, lower the level of Otis's excitement over what in the hell was happening to him with a young woman named Sharon.

The thoughts were coming like split-second rocket shots. The stockholders, policyholders, and employees of Kansas Central Fire and Casualty would most likely not stand by him the way the American people had stood by Clinton. Annabel was no Chelsea, and he knew for certain that Sally Winfield was no Hillary Rodham Clinton. What was it that Republican congressman from Texas had said when asked how his wife would react to his having an affair with a young intern type? He had said he'd be lying in a pool of blood while she asked how in the hell you reloaded this damned thing. Well, Sally would probably handle it about the same.

Why was he thinking things like that, anyhow? For chrissake, here we are, taking a little ride on a Cushman Pacemaker, not having sex—under either the Bill Clinton or the Kenneth Starr definition.

Maybe I do need some world-renowned Ashland Clinic help, thought Otis.

He stopped the scooter back near the quilt. Sharon the nurse slid off and stepped up beside him.

"All right now, Buck, take off your helmet so I can really see you," she said. "All I can tell through that face guard is that your eyes are dark and you have a mustache."

The potential for a moment of awful truth had arrived. He said nothing.

She said, "Your voice sounds very mature, Buck."

Otis raised his right hand to his helmet and gave what he considered a good imitation of a cowboy salute, something along the lines of what Red Ryder might have done. He couldn't think of anything Red Ryder ever said, so he went with what he did know: " 'From out of the past come the thundering hoofbeats of the great horse Silver—the Lone Ranger rides again! Hiii-yo, Silver, away!' "

He gunned the handlebar throttle, released the brake, and disappeared on his Cushman Pacemaker down the path, accompanied by a small amount of dust and the sounds of putt-putt-putt.

He was also moving his mouth ever so slightly while whispering—not singing—the words to the fourth verse of "Sunflower."

> Oh, the moon is brighter,
> And the stars are bluer
> And the gals are sweeter
> And their hearts are truer,
> And I'm here to state
> There's one who's really great
> She's a sunflower
> From the Sunflower State.

THREE

BOB GIDNEY HAD called it about how Sally would react to Otis's buying a Cushman. She theatened Otis. He either voluntarily went to talk to someone at the world-renowned Ashland Clinic about his problem or she would force the issue directly, through Bob and other doctors, or by some other means—gunpoint, if necessary. A *real* gun, not some kid's BB thing.

She went completely over the edge upon his return from his hour-long Sunday afternoon ride, which he had taken off on without any discussion while she was working in her rose garden in back.

And she didn't even know about his Buck-like spin with young Sharon.

"Corporate CEOs do not ride around on forty-year-old motor scooters wearing football helmets and carrying pop guns named for comic book cowboys," Sally said.

"Maybe more of them should," said Otis gamely. He laughed, trying to make a joke of it all.

Sally wasn't buying. "You go to Ashland Clinic tomorrow, or I will get it done through Pete Wetmore and the board of KCF and C if I have to. They may not want an untreated lunatic run-ning their company."

"Pete wouldn't have the sense or the courage or the guts or the smarts or the balls or the energy or the heart or the soul to do a goddamn thing," said Otis.

"He's going through the same thing you are—a midlife crisis of some kind," she replied quickly. "It has hit him a little ear-lier in life than you, and it's turned him to mush, that's all."

"He was born mush."

"Go to Ashland!" she screamed.

So he went to the world-renowned Ashland Clinic the next afternoon.

THE CLINIC WAS housed in a large mansion and several smaller buildings in a fourteen-acre wooded setting on the west side of Eureka. It resembled a rich man's estate or the campus of a small private school, both of which it had been in earlier lives. One of the founders of Eureka who had made and then lost great sums of money on the huge natural-gas fields of central Kansas and northeastern Oklahoma had built the original house as a monument to himself. His name was Sam Gulliver, and the house—a three-story twenty-seven-room brick replica of an English country home—was still known as the Gulliver House, a fact that often got kids and naive tourists thinking it was where the Gulliver of *Gulliver's Travels* lived. The place and the land had been taken over by a small Catholic girls' boarding school after World War II. They had added several buildings, and when the school went out of business in the late 1970s, the Ashland people bought it at auction for their clinic.

The Ashland founders were eight doctors and researchers from the Moran Foundation, the first of several well-known and well-regarded mental health institutions in the Midwest. The eight had a joint falling-out with the Moran leadership over Freudian theory as well as what they called "ego development" among the clinic's older establishment. They moved as a group 140 miles west from Moran, Missouri, to Eureka, Kansas, and opened Ashland Clinic, the name having come from the obscure fact that Freud had once stayed in a British country hotel named Ashland.

Dr. Clyde (Knothole) Norton was the last of the Ashland founders still alive and, at eighty-seven, continued to exercise overall control of the clinic and the foundation that ran it. Legend was that his very private nickname had been given him years ago—as a young man, he had resembled a knothole in a freshly cut cottonwood tree: small, round, woody, grainy.

Otis thought about putt-putting out to Ashland on his red motor scooter but figured that would be truly throwing a red flag in the face of the bull. So he went instead in his tan Explorer.

As arranged, Bob Gidney met Otis at the front desk and took him directly to Dr. Russell Tonganoxie, the psychiatrist Bob had touted before. Bob said Tonganoxie was known worldwide for his studies, writings, and travels in pursuit of truths about what he called "The Mature Male in Crisis."

Otis's first impression of the fifty-year-old-or-so Tonganoxie was that he had to look no further than in a mirror if he wanted to see a mature male in crisis. Russell Tonganoxie's long dark brown hair came down over his ears, and he wore his khaki chinos at least a size too large and barely pressed, as well as a gray sweatshirt with PACKERS on the front.

"Don't be put off by the way I look," he said immediately, as if he had been reading Otis's mind. "We all have our situations."

He pointed at a leather chair for Otis to sit in. The office had probably been a master bedroom in its life with the Gullivers. Lavish moldings framed the room, the ceilings were high, and a huge fireplace and mantel covered most of one wall, tall French windows another. Tonganoxie's desk was a long pine table covered with books and stacks of stapled-together papers—reports of various kinds, presumably.

Tonganoxie said, "When I came here from Johns Hopkins six months ago, I negotiated a deal. Not only no white coat but no coat of any kind, no tie. It's in my contract that I can wear to work anything I want. That was my little Eureka."

Otis said nothing.

"You *do* know what the name of your—our—town means?"

"Yes. It's Greek for 'I found it,'" said Otis matter-of-factly. "The chamber uses the phrase a lot in its promotion stuff, as do the other ten or so towns in America named Eureka." Otis was not interested in engaging in small talk with this guy. So he didn't even mention the idiot city councilman who had tried a few years back—unsuccessfully, thank God—to add an exclamation point to the official name of this Eureka, thus making Eureka!, Kansas, the only city or town in America—maybe the world—with an exclamation point in addition to a comma between its name and its state.

"What about Archimedes? Do you know a lot about Archimedes?" Tonganoxie asked.

Otis shook his head. He didn't know a lot about Archimedes.

"Well, sir, as an important citizen of this Eureka, you must surely know that Archimedes was a Sicilian-born Greek mathematician who coined that word, 'eureka,' in about the year 230 B.C. He said it after discovering for the king how much of the crown was pure gold. 'Eureka!' he yelled. 'Eureka! Eureka! I found it! I found it!' Meaning he had found the answer—"

Tonganoxie stopped talking. And when he resumed a few seconds later, he said, "All right, all right. Let's get on with trying to determine if you're sick or simply a guy hit by a routine run-of-the-mill bout of Motorcycle Syndrome."

"Motor *scooter*," Otis said. "I bought a Cushman motor scooter, not a motorcycle."

"That's too bad. There's a lot in the neurosis literature already on men in their fifties, sixties, and seventies buying motorcycles. It's quite common. As men slow down in real life, they want to do something that speeds them up. Nothing on scooters, though. Scooters—Cushman or any other kind—aren't known for their speed, are they? I wouldn't think running away from home on a scooter would work very well. I hope you're not thinking about doing anything like that. You'd have to stay off the interstates, that's for sure. The trucks would blow you off the highway. I'm a Jeep man, myself."

Otis almost said, "Jeep?" but caught himself before there was engagement.

Tonganoxie answered as if he had said it anyhow. "My dad was an army officer, and I grew up with a deep and abiding passion for the Jeep, believing it to be the finest motor vehicle ever made. I own four of them now. They range in age from fifty years to fifty days."

Otis found that interesting but still resisted a temptation to react, to participate.

Tonganoxie continued, "Wheels, there's something about wheels that turns on males. They're as much a part of our standard equipment as what's between our legs. They've done serious studies about it. UVA did one five years ago with eighty-two kids of all ages—forty-one boys, forty-one girls, of ages two to fourteen. They were put into rooms full of toys and gadgets. The boys, no matter the age, went immediately to the cars and trucks and trains and buses or whatever there was with wheels. The

4 0 | JIM LEHRER

girls didn't. A follow-up study done at Yale using bikes, cars, and pickups with college-age men and women had the same result. And there is good anecdotal evidence that the wheels thing continues right on through to the end of a man's life."

Otis, again, had no reaction. He knew from his own experience about the importance of wheels to little boys and grown men. He didn't need a shrink or a study to tell him anything else about it.

"I have my wheels," said Tonganoxie, moving on, "but I don't own a toy fire truck or a BB gun. I used to have a baseball batting helmet, but that's been a while. You've got one of those, too, is that right?"

"It's a Kansas City Chiefs *football* helmet."

"I grew up a Green Bay fan," said Tonganoxie, tapping his Packers sweatshirt. "I can't imagine ever rooting for any other team than the Packers."

Then it was back to business. Tonganoxie asked Otis to describe that first moment—the Crack Moment, he called it—when Otis had seen the toy fire engine at the antiques show.

Otis did so in a few words, and Tonganoxie asked, "Did you feel something in you go 'crack!'?"

"No," replied Otis.

"A hot flash, a feeling of well-being, a sweep of nausea, a tear, a chest pain, a wham, a crash—anything?"

"Nothing."

"Not even a little snap, crackle, or pop?"

"Not a snap, crackle, or pop."

"Had you ever had thoughts before that day about someday— any day ever in your life—buying some of the things you couldn't have as a child?"

"No."

"So it just happened?"

"It just happened."

Otis was beginning to seriously wonder how this guy ever got to be a psychiatrist, much less known in the world for anything special or important. Talking to him was like talking to the guy in line at the 7-Eleven.

That wasn't quite right. There was a lilt and an authority in Tonganoxie's voice that might have signaled some basic intelligence as well as a good sense of humor. But it was all very well disguised.

"At least you're not a Silver Star," Tonganoxie said. "At least I assume you're not. You haven't made up a phony daring bio about being a war hero or a football star, anything like that, have you?"

Otis shook his head. He had been tempted a time or two, particularly when having to explain to a room of men why a stupid injury in college had kept him out of the military.

"Silver Star Syndrome, we call it. A psychiatrist who did some work with the military borrowed the term from them. Some guys, as they age, get carried away with wishing they had done more when they were young or been braver or faster or whatever. Before they know it, instead of telling people the truth about how they spent the entire Korean War in a reserve unit at home, say, they're talking about how they won the Silver Star or some other kind of medal for taking out a Red Chinese machine-gun nest at the Chosin Reservoir. Politicians and other public figures get caught at it all the time. I've treated several Silver Stars. They're everywhere."

Otis said that was not his problem, never had been his problem, and never would be his problem.

"All right, then," said Tonganoxie. "Another common cause of the so-called Second Childhood Syndrome—no offense—is baldness. You got a problem being bald?"

Otis felt warmth in his face, which meant Tonganoxie was now seeing red in Otis's face. "Not anymore," Otis said.

"You're offended—and embarrassed—just by the question. So that tells me you've still got a problem with being bald. When did you go bald?"

"It started in my twenties."

"When did it end?"

"In my thirties."

"You're really pissed about it, aren't you?"

Otis said nothing.

"You wonder why you, huh? You see me with all of this hair, and you see other people all around you—men twice your age—with full heads of hair. Was your dad bald?"

"No."

"Either one or both of your grandfathers?"

"No."

"So, with no warning and no expectations, you were picked out at random to have no hair on your head. Makes you really want to tell the god of hair or whoever to go fuck him- or herself, doesn't it?"

Otis said, "I'm a bald-headed man. That's what I am. Can we go on to something else?"

"Sure. But you ought to know that there could be reason to believe it's your baldness that caused you to do the helmet and fire engine and motorcycle—scooter, sorry—bit. All of that stuff takes you back to a time when you had hair. Maybe you're trying to build yourself a little time capsule. If so, you're not the first. It's quite common, in fact, among bald-headed men, particularly those who hate their jobs."

Otis wanted out of here. Not in years had he wanted out of any place or situation as much as he wanted out of this one. He did not talk about being bald to anyone. It was something that had happened to him, and that was that. It was like having a terrible accident that had left him terribly scarred or deformed.

Tonganoxie said, "It's understandable, because you were robbed of some of your younger years. Being bald made you look older than your actual age. I'll bet you looked sixty when you were forty. Right?"

Otis said nothing and did nothing but stare ahead at a framed diploma on the wall.

"How old *are* you, by the way?" Tonganoxie asked.

"Fifty-nine."

"When will you be sixty?"

"In a couple of weeks or so."

"Eureka, that's it. You're now fifty-nine-year-old Otis Halstead, and soon you're going to be sixty-year-old Otis Halstead. And you hate that. At Johns Hopkins, I once treated a guy—he was a very famous Pulitzer Prize–winning newspaper editor—who was so upset about turning sixty that he wouldn't come out from under the covers the morning of his sixtieth birthday. He stayed in his bed and under those covers for forty-seven days. So, if it's approaching sixty that's triggered all of this, know for a fact that you're not the only one. And it's perfectly normal—almost."

Otis shook his head once and kept staring at the wall.

Tonganoxie let the silence lie for a good thirty seconds. Then he said, "All right, sir. I'm not bald, and I'm not sixty, but I do have my Jeeps. So I have some understanding, on a personal as well as a professional level, about what's going on—or *may* be going on. On, then, to something else. I understand you're big in the insurance business?"

Otis, desperate and delighted to move on, confessed that to be the fact.

"I'll bet you hate it, right, Otis? I'll call you Otis, you call me Russ."

"Okay, Russ. No, I don't hate it," said Otis.

"One of the most common causes of depression and suicide among aging men, particularly the successful ones, is that they hate their jobs. They've worked their asses off to get to the top, and once they get there, they hate it. But they can't say anything about it because it doesn't sound right. How can somebody be unhappy with being successful? It's tough, it's what I've spent the last several years studying. Again, I've had my own problems in this area, too. Being a shrink—don't tell Gidney I said that—isn't all peaches and cream every day, either. How many men your age do you know who are truly happy, Otis?"

When Otis failed to answer, Tonganoxie said, "I'll bet it's damned few. Isn't that a terrible thing? I sure as hell think it is."

Otis still had nothing to say.

Tonganoxie grabbed from his desk what looked like a clipping out of a magazine. "I assume you know who Anthony Hopkins is? The famous and great and extremely successful British actor? Somebody just sent me this the other day. Quote: 'I can't take it anymore . . . I have wasted my life. To hell with this stupid show business, this ridiculous showbiz, this futile wasteful life. I look back and see a desert wasteland. After thirty-five years I look back and cringe with embarrassment and say to myself: How could you have done that? I've done one or two good films and some bad films. It was a complete waste of time.' End quote. Hopkins is sixty years old. Now, that's really sad."

Otis, who had particularly admired Hopkins in *The Remains of the Day,* agreed that it was really sad.

"With you, Otis, it could also be about guilt," Tonganoxie said. "You feel guilty about being in the insurance business, right?"

"Guilty? Why in the hell should I feel guilty?"

"Aren't insurance companies really bloodsucking vultures who live off the tragedies and fears of the rest of us? Without plane crashes and fires and floods and hurricanes and heart attacks, where would you be? You must feel guilty for getting rich off the fears and tears of others. But you haven't got the guts to quit, so you've gone out and bought a lot of silly little-boy things."

Otis was furious. He stood up. "I've got better things to do with my time that having some long-haired jerk in a Packers sweatshirt mouth off about things he doesn't know a damned thing about. If I'm a bloodsucker, you're a brainsucker. Good day and go fuck-er yourself, Russ."

"Good day and go fuck-er *yourself*," Tonganoxie said with a huge smile. He did not stand up.

"Maybe it's only boring," he said as Otis arrived at the door. "All those numbers and risk analyses—reports to read, financial statements to ponder, meetings to conduct. Boring, boring, boring. You're bored. That's all it is. Not hate but boredom. More common among CEOs, even, than motorcycle fetishes."

Otis opened the door and screamed back at Tonganoxie, "Motor *scooter,* asshole!"

"On second thought, Otis, maybe you're nothing but a classic No Need Monster—"

Otis slammed the door hard behind him as he left.

OUT IN THE main hallway, there stood good Bob Gidney, trying to look like he was supposed to be there.

"Well, that didn't take long," Bob said to Otis.

"The man's an idiot," Otis said, still moving. "Did you know he owned four Jeeps? Nobody owns four Jeeps except the U.S. Army."

Bob, walking along with Otis, said, "He insulted you, right?"

"You're damned right he did."

"He always does that. What did he say?"

"He said successful people are depressed, and insurance people like me are bloodsucking vultures who feed on the tragedies of humankind. He said I should and do feel guilty about it. Or maybe I'm just bored. Or that I hate being almost sixty and bald. He's an asshole. He's the one who needs help."

Bob strode alongside Otis out the front door, down the mansion's steps toward Otis's Explorer, parked in a small graveled parking lot.

"That's Russ's technique—a form of eyeball-to-eyeball shock treatment, he calls it," Bob said. "He first pisses off the patient and then waits for him to think about it awhile, to decide he might be right after all, and then to call for another appointment to continue the discussion."

"He'd better not hold his breath for *my* call," Otis said, jumping into the Explorer and slamming the door with gusto. Then he rolled down the window and asked Bob, "Do you know a lot about Archimedes? The Greek who first said 'Eureka'?"

"All I know is that he was supposedly stepping into his bath with the king's crown. He put the crown down in the water with him and made a discovery about the weight of gold being lighter than silver. Something like that. Also, late in his life, he helped invent geometry, I think. A Roman soldier killed him. Maybe for inventing geometry, who knows. What brought that up?"

Otis didn't answer. He put the Explorer in gear. "What's a No Need Monster?"

"It's a very unprofessional nickname Tonganoxie and his fellow experts have for a particular type of depressed male."

Otis rolled up the window and gunned the engine. Bob Gidney waved goodbye.

The Explorer didn't move. Otis put the window back down and said, "Give me a thirty-second definition."

Bob said, "Ambitious young married man throws himself completely into his job so he can be a huge success, provide for his family. Wife and children are forced to make lives without him because he's never there. Then, sometime in his late forties or early fifties, the man arrives at the top, turns around to have a family life, and discovers that nobody needs him for anything except as a provider. That turns him into a depressed monster of some kind—there are several different varieties—"

Otis, without gunning the engine, eased the Explorer away at a very slow speed.

BACK AT THE clinic, Tonganoxie was still thinking about Otis Halstead.

Asshole. He called me an asshole. Maybe so—maybe right now I am. Of course, in the world of us shrinks, there is no one definition for asshole.

Russ Tonganoxie had come to Kansas alone, having left the second of two former wives and three children—two from his first marriage, one from the second—back on the East Coast in Baltimore and a Boston suburb. He had come here to the middle of nowhere mostly for professional reasons, because Ashland had offered him a deal he couldn't refuse. But on a personal level, there were problems. He had never really lived by himself, and he was already weary of the unsettling silence that greeted him at his Kansas door and at the refrigerator, at the dinner table, in the backyard, in the bathroom—in the bedroom.

All he had were his Jeeps. He kept them in the garage of his 1950s one-story brick rambler in the middle of an acre of flatland in southwest Eureka. There was the new Wrangler, which he drove to and from the clinic and around town. It was a special Sahara edition—the exterior color was officially called desert sand; the interior was camel. There was also an olive-drab original, made in 1942 in Toledo, Ohio, by Willys-Overland; it had spent World War II at Fort Benning in Georgia. The other two were a flashy red Jeepster convertible, from the late forties, and a little red-white-and-blue right-hand-drive postal Jeep from the 1960s.

Yes, he thought after Otis left, *I have my wheels, too. But not much more than that right now except for some interesting patients. First there was the number two man at the large insurance company who hates his life, and here, now, comes his boss, who seems to hate his even more.*

FOUR

THE ISSUE WAS whether KCF&C should launch a special insurance for computer-dependent businesses and industries. Otis had assigned a task force under Pete Wetmore to study the risks and feasibility of entering this new line. There was to be a full report by this afternoon.

So at 2:35, within thirty minutes after he returned from Ashland Clinic, Otis began the meeting with Pete in the executive conference room on the top floor high above downtown and all of Eureka. The fourteen-story KCF&C Building had long dominated the Eureka skyline. The building's ornate beige brick structure was the landmark toward which all eyes, traffic, and commerce moved.

Eureka was the fourth largest city in Kansas—behind Wichita, Kansas City, and Topeka. Its seventy-three thousand people in the middle of the state were a mix of professors and students at Central Kansas State College; farm boys and girls who worked at various so-called light-industry plants that did everything from make fertilizer to assemble small jitney-style buses for airport use; and well-educated white-collar folks who ran and manned KCF&C, the banks, and several sizable accounting and law firms. Ninety percent of the population was white, and 80 percent of the adults had at least a high school education. The public schools were considered among the best in the state, as were the police, the welfare system, the libraries, the health care facilities, and most everything else. Eureka, in other words, lived up to its name on most counts. And it was always easy to find, sitting in the middle of the flat prairie without even a small hill for twenty-five miles in any direction.

Mush. His and Sally's word for Pete. That was all Otis, sitting here atop Eureka, could think of as Pete talked. Mush. The man *is* mush, his mind is mush. What in the hell is this company going to do when I retire? How in the hell can this piece of mush take over the company?

Otis looked out the window to the western reaches of Eureka and beyond. Sometimes, recently, on days when he was feeling warm and well about his BB gun and toy fire truck and Cushman Pacemaker, Otis swore he could see the Grand Canyon or maybe Los Angeles, way, way out there somewhere.

Right now he swore those were the Rockies, west of Denver, that he saw on the clear blue horizon. And hey, isn't that Pagosa Springs, home of the Red Ryder museum, out there?

Pete mushed on and on: "The basis for the premise is that computers sometimes malperform or, in computer language, crash. Computer crashes can cause severe business harm and loss to a particular firm or company. A brokerage firm unable to process its stock transactions could lose millions of dollars. An airline reservation and scheduling system presents similar downside potential. So could other computer-dependent companies, of which there are an increasing number. The question is whether the rewards for us entering the field to provide computer crash insurance would outweigh the risk, and at this point, confirming data is not available. Our company has never in its history been reluctant to see new horizons, to chart new courses, to enter new and challenging fields."

Mush, mush, mush.

KCF&C was almost as much a part of Kansas as the sunflower—the flower and the song—and "Home on the Range," the official state song. The company had been founded as a cooperative in the late 1880s by several new-immigrant German farm families, most of them Mennonites. They needed protection from fire, pestilence, and the extremes of central Kansas weather for their Turkey Red wheat crops as well as their homes, implements, livestock, and other personal possessions. In the 1920s KCF&C became a mutual insurance company, with agents and farm customers all over Kansas, and then, after World War II, it reinvented itself again as a standard stockholder-owned corporation. When Otis joined the company in 1968, it had spread its reach to most of the Midwest, including both Kansas City and Chicago, where it sold auto as well as homeowners' and other kinds of insurance. Working sometimes around the clock and traveling anywhere and everywhere there was a client or a deal, Otis had expanded it further into a major national company. Was it now time to expand into computer crash insurance?

Pete mushed on: "Yes, there are possible rewards for being one of the first to enter the computer crash field, but the risks of being first at anything are always enormous. As, of course, are the rewards. The man who made the first car was richer than the man who made the last one. But the record is silent on whether there was a first man who tried to make the first car and failed before the one who actually did."

Otis kept his eyes toward the Rockies, toward the Red Ryder museum in Pagosa Springs. Did this idiot just say "The man who made the first car was richer than the man who made the last one?" What was the rest of the mush he just said about there being a first before the first? What in the hell does it have to do with insuring against computers crashing? *Where am I? What am I doing? Who is this man speaking? Why is he mush?*

How and where are you, Sharon?

Pete kept talking. "We have drawn some actuarial paradigms and underwriting and probability markups and patterns and projections and predictions and contingencies and mutual benefits and premium and business plans and spreadsheets and test runs and play-outs and CD-ROMS and PBCs and AFCPs and huddles and puddles and cookouts and drive-bys and drive-ins and floppies and hard drives and end runs and home runs and piss pots and condoms and Cheerios and popcorn and playbooks and game films and Beethovens and Bachs and calculus and algebra and trigonometry and 747s and Count Basies . . ."

Otis glanced across the table at Pete, who was also staring off to the West, toward the Rockies, Pagosa Springs, the Grand Canyon, and Los Angeles.

". . . and trumpets and pancakes and maple syrup and claims and innovations and income potentials and downsides and upsides and tanning salons and Exercycles and jogging."

Pete stopped talking, and Otis turned back to face the West. Neither man said a word. The silence grew.

Otis had never been present when another human being really lost it, came unglued, went over the top. He had the feeling he was having his first such experience.

Pete said, "I hate the insurance business, Otis."

Otis, still looking west, said, "Why, Pete?"

"We're bloodsuckers, Otis. We make it on the backs of the lame and hurt and dead and deprived."

"Bullshit, Pete. We help the lame, hurt, dead, and deprived. We help them get through their crises. We give them a sense of security and comfort, and we give them money."

"Whatever. It's also boring as hell. I haven't had a fun day here at the office since the first day two years, nine months, and two days ago, when you took me around and introduced me to everybody. That was the high point of my career at KCF and C. What kind of fucking commentary on my life is that?"

Silence again for a while.

Pete said, "I'm not going to get your job when the time comes, am I?"

Otis had to make a decision. Tell the truth now or later? *When do I put this man out of his misery? Now? Yes.*

"Most likely, you're not, that's right," he said.

"You shouldn't have hired me in the first place. Why did you?"

"These things are hard to explain when they don't work out—"

"It was my fault. I never should have taken this fucking job. I knew this wasn't for me. I knew it, I knew it."

Otis elected not to comment on that. He let it sit there and then said, "When you were a kid, what did you want to grow up to be?"

"A trumpet player in Count Basie's band."

"I didn't even know you played the trumpet, Pete."

"I won the Colorado state championship for the trumpet, and I played in dance bands around Boulder and Fort Collins. I played once at the Brown Palace Hotel in Denver with the Glenn Miller Orchestra—there still was one for years after he died in that plane crash, you know. The Brown Palace was and is the best hotel in Colorado. The band leader—I forget his name—said I had one of the best sets of natural-born trumpet lips he had ever seen."

Pete fell silent. After several seconds, Otis, still not looking at Pete, asked, "Why didn't you pursue the trumpet?"

"My dad was a car dealer, and he wanted me to be the lawyer he never was, and then I married June while still in college and she was pregnant by the time the honeymoon was over and we had Josephine and then the twins and then Bobby, and the life of a trumpet player was not for all of that. What did you want to be when you grew up, Otis? President and CEO of a fucking insurance company in Eureka, Kansas?"

"I've never heard you use 'fucking' before, Pete."

"I've never used it in front of you before, that's why."

Otis noticed that the mushiness had disappeared. Pete's voice was now hearty, robust, direct. Alive. Here in the middle of talking about insuring crashing computers, the man had come alive and gone nuts at the same time.

Otis said, "To answer your question, I wanted to be Johnny Mercer."

"I never got into baseball. Was he a shortstop for the Cardinals?" Pete said.

"Johnny Mercer wasn't a ballplayer, goddammit, he was a singer and songwriter. How could you know music and not know about him?"

Otis waited for a follow-up question such as "What songs did he write or sing?" Something. He kept talking about Johnny Mercer whether Pete cared or not.

"Johnny wrote more than a thousand songs—pop songs, famous pop songs. Mostly just the lyrics. Everything from 'Autumn Leaves,' 'Laura,' and 'Fools Rush In' to 'Jeepers Creepers,' 'I'm an Old Cowhand,' and 'Ac-cent-tchu-ate the Positive,' 'Moon River,' even—with Mancini."

"That was my favorite song for a while," Pete said.

Otis assumed he meant "Moon River," which was a lot of people's favorite song. It made many men think of Audrey Hepburn in *Breakfast at Tiffany's.*

But Pete had another song in mind. In a quiet, unmelodic monotone, he talked-sang:

"I'm an old cowhand,
From the Rio Grande,
But my legs aren't really bowed,
And my cheeks ain't tan,
'Cause I ride the place in a Ford V-8,
I know ever road in the Lone Star State,
Yippie-yi-yo-ki-yay,
Yippie-yi-yo-ki-yay . . ."

Otis picked up the few word errors and omissions in the way Pete recited the lyrics. But there was no point in correcting Pete. He was pretty close.

Pete said, "I sang that as a kid with my brother and two uncles when we wanted to act like cowboys. I may have known then that Johnny Mercer had written it, but I had forgotten him. Now that you mention it, didn't he also write the Santa Fe railroad song?"

Otis nodded. Yes, yes, Johnny Mercer wrote "On the Atchison, Topeka and the Santa Fe." Otis had sung it in high school with a perfect replica of a Mercer twang—southern, a bit nasal—that had brought him to wanting to actually *be* Johnny Mercer.

Pete didn't ask Otis any further questions, such as: What happened? Why didn't you become Johnny Mercer? It was a story Otis had told no one, not even Sally. But he might have at this moment told Pete if he had asked.

Instead, Pete said, "So here we sit. A failed trumpet player and a failed Johnny Mercer, talking about whether we should insure people's fucking computers."

"*Crashing* fucking computers, Pete."

"I wish I had something like a Cushman obsession to fall back on—to occupy me—like you do."

"There's nothing you wanted as a kid that you couldn't have?"

"Nothing. I got everything I wanted. Everything."

Otis felt and heard movement and turned toward Pete, who was standing.

"I'm out of here, Otis. I'm gone—forever. I'm not even going back to my office. I'm going to the elevator and out of this building and never coming back. Please have my personal effects and any money owed me from profit-sharing and all the rest sent to June at the house. Thanks for everything."

"Wait a minute, my friend," Otis said, on his feet and moving around the table.

"We're not friends," Pete said. "You always treated me like shit, like I was a goddamned idiot."

"Until right now, that's about what I thought you were. I'm sorry, but that's the truth."

"Goodbye, Otis."

"Let me help you. You ought to talk to somebody."

"One of those fucking shrinks at Ashland everybody in Eureka talks to all the time? I've done that, thanks. They're crazier than the rest of us."

Otis said, "What about a trumpet? Go buy yourself a trumpet, Pete. Right now. Go right now and buy a trumpet."

Pete smiled, said, "Whatever you say, Mr. Johnny Mercer," and left the room.

ONCE THE DOOR was shut, Otis said softly to the West:

"Do you hear that whistle down the line?
I figure that it's engine number forty-nine.
She's the only one that'll sound that way,
On the Atchison, Topeka and the Santa Fe . . ."

He did not sing the words in a Johnny Mercer voice. He only spoke them in an Otis Halstead voice.

And then he sat motionless, silently looking west, for nearly thirty minutes.

He thought about Pete and whether he should go find him and talk to him some more. And he thought about the Cushman and Johnny Mercer and that young nurse named Sharon and about profanity.

He thought about being fifty-nine-year-old—soon-to-be-sixty-year-old—Otis Halstead. At least he was no Silver Star. He had always told everybody the truth about his washing out of naval ROTC and a military commitment by a stupid accident in college. He probably could have gotten away with telling people he had been a navy officer who commanded patrol boats in Vietnam or something. Nobody would have checked. But that kind of stuff was not for him, Otis the responsible son, husband, father, businessman. And friend?

No, not friend. No friend to Pete, for sure. Pete was right about that. *I really did—do—treat the poor bastard like shit. But goddammit, how could I have known the guy was moving ever so slowly but surely toward a breakdown? Mush is mush, shit is shit. I'm no world-famous Ashland Clinic shrink.*

Otis decided against going after Pete right now. Or calling somebody at Ashland or even down the hall in Pete's office. Pete will walk it off, think it off. He'll be fine. With his background and education, how can he be anything but fine? Maybe he really will go and buy a trumpet.

Otis finally returned to his own office on the penthouse floor. It was a large place filled mostly with designer-selected paintings of still lifes and heavy dark brown furniture that fit the heaviness of his CEO position. Otis had never taken the time to really personalize this space where he spent so many of his days and nights.

He looked through some monthly sales reports. The Omaha/ Lincoln district was down again—more than 10 percent over February. Don Caney, the district manager, wasn't making it. Time maybe coming soon to move him back to the home office in the underwriting department, where he started and belonged. There are salesmen and there is everybody else. Caney was an everybody else. Chicago/Peoria was up. Good, good. So was Wichita/Oklahoma City. He checked the insurance categories companywide. A little burst of activity in boat insurance. There had better be. There was always an increase in boat insurance sales in the spring as people got ready for summer.

Then he glanced at some new data from one of the insurance industry's research institutes. Mandatory air bags for all seats in all cars and vehicles were coming, and the prospect was to save three thousand lives and $21.4 million a year for the insurance industry. Hip, hip, hooray.

There was another *Our Future* report to peruse. The crashing-computer task force had come from such a report. This one had to do with KCF&C entering the banking business if and when the U.S. Congress and others permitted insurance companies to do so. Some believed there was a great future out there for the insurance company that turned itself into a full-service one-stop financial center. Maybe so, maybe someday.

Otis's secretary, a sharp and unassuming woman of forty-five from western Kansas named Melissa, inquired on the intercom about Pete Wetmore. She said Mr. Wetmore's secretary had not seen him since he left to attend the conference room meeting with Otis two hours ago. Pete had said to tell her that an emergency had come up and that he'd decided to leave for the day. Nothing to worry about.

Otis picked up his phone and called Bob Gidney at the Ashland Clinic. Otis figured Bob thought Otis was calling to set up another appointment with Russ Tonganoxie. No, said Otis, he had a question.

"Is there some kind of mental disorder that causes people to suddenly start saying 'fucking' all the time?"

"Not just that word but all kinds of foul things—whatever comes into the mind comes out the mouth," Bob said. "It's called Tourette's syndrome, named for a French physician in the late 1880s."

"Is it very serious?"

"Not necessarily—usually only very embarrassing. Have you come down with it?"

"No. But I think a colleague of mine may have."

"Who?"

"That's none of your 'fucking' business."

Otis hung up and had a brief second thought or two about whether he should have said something specific to Bob about Pete. Not just about "fucking" but about his trumpet frustration, his troubled thoughts, his walking away from his office and job—his losing it right there in front of Otis.

But Pete said he had already talked to the people at Ashland. Forget it.

Otis saw from his watch that it was almost five o'clock. He picked up a file folder from an executive placement firm in Chicago—headhunters, they were called—that he had contacted secretly to begin looking for a new number two. He had concluded for sure a few months ago that Pete Wetmore definitely was not going to make it. The board had pushed Otis to have a natural and agreed-to succession in place before he was contemplating retirement. So, assuming he stuck with it until he was sixty-five, he still had some time to get things lined up.

The file had the photos and bios and dossiers on two men—both white baby boomers in their mid-forties, both now working for giant insurance companies in second- or third-level positions. One was a New Yorker with an MBA from Wharton, the other a Californian who had started in the business as a company lawyer. Both were married with young children, both took good photographs.

Both, on paper, came across a lot better than Pete Wetmore did before Otis had hired him.

But maybe Pete might make it after all. Maybe he could work his way out of the mush.

Otis heard a loud scream outside. Before he could really react, Melissa burst through the door. She had her hands up to her face.

"It's Mr. Wetmore! They just found him in his car! He's dead!"

PETE AND JUNE Wetmore's home was only six blocks west of the Halsteads in NorthPark, their upscale residential enclave. It consisted of some thirty houses of varying motifs—English Georgian, French château, Tuscan villa, Spanish castle, Cape Cod tony, Miami Beach deco, Jacobsen white, Southampton beachy, and so on—along a series of carefully drawn winding streets and cul-de-sacs. No matter the style, each house sat amid at least a half acre of trees on acre-plus lots, and most had swimming pools, three-car-plus garages, and sweeping circular driveways.

The Wetmores' house was a light beige Spanish-castle design. Otis had been there only once or twice, but as he drove up to it now, he had no question which one it was.

There were two police cars and several other cars in the driveway and out front. Clearly, something was going on here. The front door was slightly ajar, and Otis walked on in. He heard soft voices coming from the living room on the left.

He stepped to the room's threshold and saw maybe twenty-five people in the room. Everyone was standing and speaking quietly, mostly in small groups. Some were familiar faces. The first he acknowledged was Sally's. He had called her from the office and suggested she go over to be with June Wetmore.

"June treated me coldly and very rudely, Otis," Sally said after motioning him to one side. "She kept mumbling something about all of this being 'your son-of-a-bitch husband's fault.' Meaning you, of course."

Yes, meaning me, of course, Otis thought.

"Her kids are upstairs with some relatives, and she's in another room now with Josh Garnett." Josh was the pastor of the First Methodist Church of Eureka, where both the Halsteads and the Wetmores were members. "But when you do see June, don't be surprised if she takes out after you. I don't know how to say it, but she acted like she hated you."

Otis said he would not be surprised. Then he moved over to another familiar face, that of Jerry Elkhart, the Cushman-loving detective who'd been at the Halstead house the afternoon Otis had returned from Nebraska with the scooter.

"I figured you'd be here," said Elkhart. "How's the scooter?"

Otis said the scooter was fine. He asked the detective exactly what had happened to Pete Wetmore. All Otis knew when he left the office was that Pete had killed himself.

"A jogger found him sitting in his car in the parking lot behind the civic auditorium. He had fired one shot from a nine-millimeter Beretta into his mouth. The medical examiner says he's one hundred percent sure it was suicide."

Elkhart held out a small white sealed envelope toward Otis. "There were two of these on the car seat next to him. One of

them had his wife's name on it. I gave it to her already. The other
was for you."

Otis took the white envelope and put it in a suit-coat pocket
without looking at it.

"Aren't you going to read it?" asked the detective.

"Not right now, if you don't mind."

The detective said he would eventually like to know what it
said, although he doubted the coroner would need any further
confirmation that Pete Wetmore had died by his own hand.

He said to Otis, "I understand you had a long private meeting with Mr. Wetmore right before he left your building to go
kill himself. Is that right?"

Otis confirmed that.

"Did he act like he was a man about to take his own life?"

"Certainly not," Otis said. "There was no question Pete was
upset about some things that had gone badly in his life. But suicide? Certainly not."

What else could I say? thought Otis. *If I had thought there was a
chance Pete was going to kill himself, I would have done something to
stop it. I would have gone after him. I would have talked him out of it.
Certainly not—that's my answer, the only possible answer.*

"One interesting thing about how he did it," said the detective. "He didn't open his mouth and stick the barrel in. He fired
it right through his lips, which appeared to be closed tight. Tore
them to shreds."

At that moment Otis noticed a trumpet lying on an end table
next to Elkhart. "Where did that come from?" Otis asked.

"It was on the car seat with the notes. Mrs. Wetmore said she'd
never seen it. We're still piecing it together, but it looks like Mr.
Wetmore went from your office building to Wellington's music
store and bought this trumpet. A while later, he went to the

parking lot of the coliseum. His wife said he always kept the Beretta in his car. That's all I know."

Two more familiar faces were next to Otis. They were those of Bob Gidney and Russ Tonganoxie, the good man and the asshole, respectively, of the world-famous Ashland Clinic. Otis turned toward them as the detective stepped away.

"Pete was a patient of yours, I take it?" Otis said to Tonganoxie, still dressed as if he were a slovenly graduate student. The only addition was a dark green warm-up jacket with the word JEEP over the breast pocket.

"I'm not permitted to discuss such things," said Tonganoxie, "and you know that."

"I guess you told Pete the same thing you told me: People in the insurance business were bloodsucking vultures who should feel guilty. Good work, Doctor."

Bob Gidney said, "This is no time to talk about anything like that, Otis. Was Pete the colleague you called me about—the cussing one?"

"I'm not permitted to discuss such things, either," said Otis.

"The immediate problem for all of us—me, you, Otis," said Tonganoxie, "is June Wetmore."

The room went suddenly silent. June Wetmore came in with the Reverend Joshua Garnett, a dull, grinning man about Otis's age.

Otis turned toward June, and their eyes met and locked. She came right toward him, her face ablaze.

"Get out of my house!" she screamed at Otis. "You drove Pete to this! You took everything out of him, you treated him like dirt!"

Shit. I treated him like shit. Not dirt, Otis thought.

Otis said nothing to her or to anyone else as he backed out of the room and left the house. Sally joined him in the front seat of the Explorer.

"I'm so sorry, darling," she said, taking Otis's right hand in both of hers. "She's just upset—understandably. Bob assures me she'll be sorry when she realizes how awful and unfair she was to you."

Otis said, "Pete left me a note. I've got it here in my pocket. I haven't read it yet."

Sally released his hand. He took out the envelope, opened it, and pulled out a folded piece of notepaper. It was a KCF&C memo sheet with Pete's name printed on the top in small letters. PETER L. WETMORE, EXECUTIVE VICE PRESIDENT.

There were only four hand-printed sentences on the sheet. Otis recognized Pete's handwriting.

Otis—
I bought a trumpet and tried to play it. But the good lips were gone. It was too late.
    Sing, Otis, sing.

                                              Pete

RUSS TONGANOXIE DEFINITELY did not want to be alone with Bob Gidney right now. But they had raced from the clinic to the Wetmores' in Tonganoxie's Jeep Wrangler, and there was no way to avoid driving back together.

He decided on a preemptive strike. "No, I didn't think Pete Wetmore was suicidal," Tonganoxie said after several moments of silence. "If I had, I would have taken direct action."

"Hey, Russ, nobody's immune from this. A patient walks out of a routine therapy session after talking about his mother and shoots up a post office with a machine gun. That kind of thing happens to all of us."

Well, fine, thought Tonganoxie. *But it's never happened quite like this to me before, and I don't want to talk about it.* But Bob Gidney was forcing him to. "I put him on Prozac, but my guess is that he didn't take much of it. I was still getting to the bottom of his neuroses."

"How depressed was he?"

"Enough to blow his brains out, obviously, for chrissake! I just didn't know it!"

Bob did not respond to the outburst, either with words or with a look.

Tonganoxie gunned the Wrangler as fast as he dared. It was only two miles or so to the clinic, but he wanted this trip to end as quickly as possible.

There was Locust Street and the gate to Ashland. Only a few more seconds now.

"Do you need to talk to someone, Russ?" Bob said as they approached the staff parking lot.

"You mean as a patient overcome with feelings of guilt or as a staff member who screwed up?" Russ asked.

"Only as a patient. As in 'Doctor, heal thyself.' "

Tonganoxie braked to a halt on the gravel of the parking lot. "I believe I can think through this on my own, but thanks, Bob," he said as he began thinking.

"What about Otis?" Bob asked as they walked toward the clinic's main building.

"What about him?"

"Is *he* liable to do something rash? Clinically abnormal?"

"No way."

FIVE

"WILL YOU GO with me?" Otis asked.

"You mean on another ride?" Sharon asked.

"A longer one this time."

"How long?"

"Oh, maybe to Hutchinson, Dodge City, Garden City, and beyond—the Rockies, the Red Ryder museum in Pagosa Springs, Colorado—or until we get tired."

"Are you out of your mind?"

It was Sunday, just after eleven in the morning. Otis had told Sally he had a splitting headache and was unable to go to church this morning. She had said that was too bad because a little church might be particularly helpful in getting him over the terrible week of Pete's suicide and the aftermath. He had agreed with that probability but said he was afraid he would be unable to keep his head up and he might even possibly throw up on the people in the pew in front of him.

"Sounds like spinal meningitis," she had said.

"No, just a simple stress headache," he had replied.

So Sally Halstead had gone to the garage, gotten in her BMW, and driven to the First Methodist Church by herself for one of the few Sundays ever, except when Otis was sick or out of town.

A few minutes later, Otis had gone to the same garage, put on his Kansas City Chiefs helmet, hung his Daisy air rifle by the lanyard to his Cushman Pacemaker motor scooter, and driven off toward Farnsworth Creek.

And there Sharon was in the same place, on the same quilt, but instead of reading a book, she was wearing earphones connected to a small yellow portable tape player beside her.

Otis stopped his scooter in the same place he had a week ago. He saw the case for the tapes. They were the companions to Beschloss's book.

Sharon, as beautiful as before, saw him shortly after he pulled up. She took off her headphones and stood up.

He immediately made the suggestion that they go off together that drew her response.

"Yes, I probably am out of my mind," he said now.

"I don't know you—I don't even know what you really look like. Are you ever going to take off that silly safety helmet?"

"It's an official Kansas City Chiefs football helmet," Otis said, unsnapping the chin strap.

She reached out toward him. Otis froze, and before he realized what she was doing, she had hold of the helmet.

"No," he said, but he made no effort to resist. This had to happen.

"Yes," she said and jerked the helmet off his head.

The look on her face was about what he'd expected. It was that of a person who had seen something truly unexpected, stunning, horrible, despicable.

Within moments Otis had his helmet back on his bald head, and he and his scooter were putt-putting alone back up the gravel path. At the blacktop, instead of turning left to go back to town, he went right, toward the West.

Sing, Otis, sing.

His initial interest in "Sunflower" and other pop songs had intensified in the ninth grade, when he was also memorizing the capitals of all the states. That had led Otis to create helpful silly ditties that were meant to be sung like the old radio jingles for cornflakes and other tasty products. He'd begun with the goal of writing a jingle for each of the then forty-eight states and their capitals, but he had done only eleven or twelve—all written in a small, blue-lined-paper spiral notebook—by the time he got tired of the enterprise.

He suddenly remembered one of them.

If I loved Ida of Boise,
And she had weeds in her garden there,
I would go and help Ida-hoe.

It was silly and stupid, but it made him laugh out loud, something he had not done in a very long time.

It had been so long, in fact, that he couldn't even remember the last time.

IT WAS NOT a sudden, spontaneous decision to turn west. He essentially made it on Thursday afternoon, on the ride from the Cottonwood Valley Cemetery after Pete Wetmore was laid to rest. Otis was in the fourth car in the funeral motorcade to and from the cemetery, well behind and away from the mortuary limos with June and the rest of the Wetmore family and close friends.

June Wetmore's anger had kept Otis far from her and everything having to do with the death of her husband. The eulogy at the funeral was given by a man who had grown up with Pete in Colorado. He spoke mostly of Pete as a kid, as a hardworking, smart, fun person who wanted to play in the Count Basie band.

Two of the eight pallbearers were from KCF&C but they were Jack Thayer, the chairman of the board, and Leonard LaCrosse, the vice president of actuarial affairs.

Otis, anonymously through Thayer, had made the suggestion that they might want to have a trumpet solo played at the funeral service. Otis sat with Sally in the back row of the church during the service. There was no trumpet solo, only the choir of the First Methodist Church singing regular funeral hymns.

Sally did her best to comfort Otis about June Wetmore's reaction toward him. So did Bob Gidney. They had obviously talked about it. Both said it was an understandable lashing-out. Bob said suicide of a loved one, particularly a spouse, can be inexplicable, but it can also overwhelm the survivor with debilitating waves of guilt. Why didn't I see it coming? Why didn't I do more to prevent it? It was my fault, it was my fault. If only I had been a better wife—or husband or son or daughter or friend—he/she would be alive today. Having another villain to share the blame helps ease the guilt.

"You are that villain on two counts, probably," said Bob. "First, for the way you treated Pete; second, for not reacting to Pete's leaving that meeting and your building that day. It will pass with time—but it will take time."

Otis doubted it would ever pass, that there would ever be enough time.

But he had also tried very hard to believe he was not the real villain, no matter what he did or didn't do. Otis knew about the trumpet, about something that had happened to Pete Wetmore many years ago. Yes, yes—Otis wished like hell that he had not treated Pete Wetmore like shit and that he had figured it was important to keep Pete in the office that fateful day. But that didn't make Otis Pete's killer.

Those lips had killed him.

On the other hand, aren't there one helluva lot of frustrated trumpet players and Johnny Mercers and opera singers and novelists and brain surgeons and pro quarterbacks and Bill Gateses who don't kill themselves? Don't they do other things to compensate, to make life work for them? Sally, for instance. She put aside her actress dreams to be a good wife and mother.

FRIDAY AFTERNOON, LATE, Otis walked from his office two blocks over to his bank and withdrew five thousand dollars in cash from his savings account. Otis was on the board of the bank, and the president, Nick Merriam, asked no questions. Otis Halstead wanted some cash, Otis Halstead got some cash—two inch-and-a-half stacks of fifties and hundreds, each held snugly and neatly by a large tan rubber band. Both knew, without having to confirm or comment, that nobody would have to be told about Otis's money, which he walked out with in a small black canvas valise he'd brought from his office.

Saturday morning, while Sally went out to run some errands, Otis placed that valise in the bottom of the spacious rear storage compartment of the Cushman. On top of the money, he stuck Jockey shorts and skivvy shirts, a pair of khaki pants, two long-sleeved shirts, a Windbreaker, gloves, a pair of heavy walking shoes, and a Dopp kit with a safety razor, toothbrush, and other basic toiletries. On top, he placed his box of BBs, maps of Kansas and the western states, and the toy fire engine.

His plan to leave on Sunday was all due to Sharon and the possibilities and his stupid thoughts and fantasies about her. He convinced himself that there was an outside chance—a one-in-a-million chance, for sure, but a chance nevertheless—that she might, on impulse, go with him. Why not delay things twenty-four hours and see for sure?

Otherwise, he would go through life wondering: *What if I had gone back to the creek and she was there and she had come with me on the scooter? I'll never know if I don't try.*

He thought of it even in the what-if context of Pete and his trumpet.

He somehow knew that he would have to take off his Chiefs football helmet. She would see him as he really was, a bald old man with a mustache. It was absolutely stupid to think that a beautiful young woman would, just like that, pick up and leave with any man she had spent only twenty minutes with, much less an ugly old one.

But she *had* returned to Farnsworth Creek. And she *was* listening to the LBJ tapes, as he had suggested. Then she saw the real him, and that was that.

At least he came and did it. It was no surprise that she said no thanks to going west with him. She wasn't crazy. But now, as his Cushman Pacemaker putt-putted along Meridian Avenue toward old U.S. Highway 56, he was at least free forever from having to think of one particular what-if in his fifty-nine years of life.

Soon to be sixty.

And he remembered another of his states ditties.

If I loved Tillie of Trenton,
and she lost or tore her shirt,
I'd buy her a New Jersey.

OTIS DIDN'T NEED to be told by Russ Tonganoxie or anyone else to stay off the interstates if he ran away from home on his Cushman.

Once he was out of the Eureka city limits and immediate suburbs, it was perfect, exactly as he'd imagined it would be here on old U.S. 56. There was only a handful of vehicles on the road, most of them old cars and pickups moving ever so slowly. The road itself was so underutilized and ignored that there were tufts of grass growing up between the cracks in places. The few people who passed or saw him as he putt-putted by smiled and waved. They apparently didn't seem to think it was particularly odd to see, on this old road, a man in a Kansas City Chiefs helmet poking along on an ancient Cushman motor scooter with a BB gun strapped to its side.

The highway, paralleling some of what had been the original Santa Fe Trail, was once part of a major network of east-west highways that cars, trucks, and buses used to traverse the United States. After the coming of the interstate across central Kansas, 56 no longer bore an official number or designation of any kind, and only the counties and towns it passed through provided maintenance and acknowledgment of its existence. Rand McNally and other makers of Kansas maps had years ago downgraded it from a solid red line to a tiny blue line.

All at once Otis was struck by being alone out on this road. Completely alone. There was nobody riding in a car with him, sitting across a desk or office or room from him, sleeping in the same bed with him, walking down a street or through a shopping mall or hotel lobby with him. Alone. *I, Otis Halstead, am alone,* he thought. *There's not even a voice from a radio or a television or a telephone. It's just me and this motor scooter and this old highway and wherever and whoever and whatever lie ahead. Have I ever been this alone?*

Then it started raining.

First just a few large drops came down, but the sky turned darker, and he could see that heavier rain was up ahead of him, right where he was going. Bad weather was not something Otis had considered very seriously. The scooter had a plastic windscreen, but it was neither large nor strong enough to keep the wet off his face or clothes. The Windbreaker he had packed wouldn't be any help at all. There was not even any point in getting it out.

The rain whipped right through the opening in the helmet into his eyes and nose and mouth. Soon water was splashing up on him from the roadway, too. He wondered how the little motor on the forty-year-old Cushman putt-putting along under him might do when it was wet.

He began to look for a place to pull over. But the road provided few of the standard places to find refuge in a downpour. There were no brightly lit Mobil or Texaco minimarts, no McDonald's or Wendy's or other fast-food restaurants, no sparkling new Comfort Inns or Days Inns along this roadside. The only eating places were those where slowness and grease still reigned, and there were no motels of any kind or quality, only decaying skeletons of those made up of a tiny office and a string of even smaller wooden cabins.

The other problem was that it was Sunday. Out on the interstate, everything was open all the time, but back down here on old U.S. 56, Sunday was still viewed as a day off.

Otis felt the scooter falter. And he heard the motor miss. The poor little old thing was drowning out. He shoved the handlebar throttle forward. He heard and felt sputtering from down below.

And then it went silent. The motor had stopped running. He turned the handlebars to the right and let the scooter coast as best as it could through puddles onto what appeared to be a large driveway. Somewhere at the end—twenty or so yards away—was a structure of some kind. He saw a light on. Was it a store? A house? Through the rain and the darkened sky, he could not tell for sure.

He dismounted and pushed the scooter on toward the light. The rain was still coming down, but there was no wind, so it was falling straight down. And it hadn't picked up in intensity. A couple of blessings.

The building seemed to be some type of combo—part run-down white frame house on the left, part shop made of gray concrete blocks on the right.

Then Otis saw in hand-painted red lettering over a large garage door on the front of the shop: CHURCH KEY CHARLIE BLUE'S FACTORY—NO CREDIT CARDS.

Otis, still pushing the scooter, continued toward the light. He knocked on the only door, which was barely above ground level, and waited.

Nothing happened. He thought he heard something inside— voices and shouting—a television set or a radio. Somebody was listening to or watching something in there.

Otis banged on the door again, this time much harder.

In a few seconds, the door swung open, and there stood one very large, very scary man.

"Who and what are you?" said the man after a quick, harsh glance at Otis, who was also almost blown away by the smell of beer coming from the man's mouth. His words were spoken in what, to Otis's Kansas ear, sounded like pure Oklahoma-Texas hillbilly.

He was a giant, a real-life giant, who clearly needed a shave, a haircut, and a bath. Otis figured him to be at least six-four and to weigh at least three hundred pounds. His hair was a barnyard blond, and it was long and uncombed and unclean. He was dressed only in a pair of filthy tent-sized work pants that, sometime in their life, may have been khaki-colored. His bare chest was huge and hairy and, like his arms and hands, smeared here and there with dark blotches that resembled grease and dirt. Otis could only guess his age. Forty? Forty-five?

"My scooter's motor drowned out," said Otis. He began to shiver, and he honestly didn't know if it was out of fear or being wet.

The man shook his head in disgust and said, "I'm closed—it's Sunday, for chrissake. The Raiders are on against the Steelers."

Otis, the rain still falling on him, stood to one side and shoved his Pacemaker in front of the door.

"That's a goddamn old thing—my cousin had one," said the man. "No wonder it quit on ya."

Now what? thought Otis.

Said the man, "Well, 'least you got wheels. I got no wheels of no kind—no car, no truck, no bike, no roller skates, no red wagon, no nothing."

With his huge right hand, he reached out, grabbed the scooter by the handlebars, and jerked it inside the house as if it were a flyweight running back. To Otis, he said, "Get your butt in here before you drown out, too."

Otis, his mind racing with uncertainty and anxiety, got his butt in there and then stood with his motor scooter, both of them dripping water on the man's floor.

But the guy didn't seem to notice or mind. He said, "The Raiders are about to score—less than a minute to the half. Find yourself a place to squat."

Otis looked around for such a place. It wasn't going to be easy.

"And take off that goddamn Chiefs helmet!" the man yelled back at Otis. "I hate the goddamn Chiefs!"

Otis took off his helmet and cradled it under his right arm. He discovered that the top of his head was about all there was on him that was dry. So there was finally some good news: Official NFL Kansas City Chiefs helmets don't leak.

As he walked around, Otis spotted another official NFL helmet. It was the familiar silver and blue of the Dallas Cowboys, and it was sitting on the floor against the far wall with what looked like a few small silver and gold trophies.

The house, if that was what it really was, was basically one square twenty-by-twenty room. There were a few open doors going off in various directions, presumably to closets or a bathroom, but what Otis saw was an unmade double bed in one corner; a couch and an easy chair in another corner, where the man was sitting in front of his television; a table and chairs, a refrigerator, a hot plate, and a sink in another. The fourth corner was filled with stacks of newspapers and magazines, framed photographs and posters. There were no rugs on the unpainted wood floor.

The place had a strange, out-of-place, unidentifiable, but nice smell—almost sweet.

"Throw it out of bounds!" the man yelled at the television. Around his feet were various sports sections of newspapers and at least a dozen empty beer bottles and cans.

The "less than a minute to the half" was in football time. Including time-outs with commercials, it was almost three minutes before the man came back to Otis and his scooter, both still dripping inside the front door.

"Want a beer?" said the man, emptying the one he had in his hand.

Otis was not a beer drinker. He preferred white wine and vodka in the summer, red wine and Scotch in the winter, but he wasn't about to decline the offer. "Sure, thanks," he said.

The man motioned for Otis to follow him over to the refrigerator. It was a badly scarred white Kelvinator with rounded corners. Otis estimated its age to be about the same as the man's—forty-plus, at least. Inside there was mostly beer, cans and bottles of Great America beer. There were also some bottles of ketchup and mustard and a few other containers and uncovered plates of leftover salads and frozen dinners and sandwiches and pieces of meat and potatoes that Otis tried not to look at very closely.

The man grabbed two dark brown bottles. He handed one of them to Otis and then turned back to a cardboard box on the floor next to the refrigerator and came up with a small silver bottle opener—a church key, as they were sometimes called. "Have one of these, too, on me," he said, handing the church key to Otis. "They used to be my stock-in-trade. Pull-tops killed it all. My name's Charlie. You may have known me as Charlie Blue—Church Key Charlie Blue."

Otis thought about that for a few beats. He remembered the sign out front. Something about Church Key Charlie Blue's Factory. But nothing else came to mind.

"Tight end, Eagles, Rams, Cowboys—two-time second-team all-pro, three-time pro bowl," said Charlie, clearly annoyed that Otis didn't remember him.

"Oh, sure, you bet," Otis lied. "You were great."

"What's your name, scooter man?"

"Otis."

"Don't lie to me, Otis. You just did about knowing who I was. I really hate people who lie to me. And everybody I ever knew did. What the fuck were you doing out there in the rain on a pussy motor scooter, Otis?"

Charlie began moving back toward the television. Otis fell in behind him and, without thinking much about it, said, "Running away. I was running away."

"From cops or women or bills? Got to be one or the other, scooter man Otis."

Charlie turned down the sound on the television and sat in

the chair, which was faded red, quilted, overstuffed. He pointed at the couch, which more or less matched. Otis sat down. He was still wet, though no longer dripping. But the room was warm, and he was also no longer shivering.

Otis wanted to answer Charlie's question but couldn't think of what to say. What, exactly, was he running away from?

Charlie said, "What are ya, Otis? Oat-tus. Sounds like a goddamn geometry teacher's name. Never figured out the point of it or algebra."

Otis had a crazy urge to say, Hey, Charlie, do you know who Archimedes was? He was the Sicilian-born Greek mathematician who first screamed "eureka," as in the name of Eureka, Kansas. He also helped invent geometry, Charlie. What do you think of that?

Instead, he said, "I'm in—*was,* I guess—insurance."

"I have been screwed, rued, and tattooed by more insurance companies than there are fizz bumps in this bottle of beer. They never want to pay up."

Charlie reached over and turned the TV back up. The halftime show was on. Four grinning, hyper men were sitting at a desk, showing highlights of games and talking endlessly and mindlessly about it all.

Charlie let them talk for a minute or two and lowered the sound and said to Otis, "They humped me out of every one of those kind of jobs. I should be doing that halftime stuff, Monday-night football, color talk, sideline shit. I could have done it better than these assholes. Look at 'em grinning and laughing at each other. They think they know football. They don't know shit. I know football. They're pulling down a mil or more a year, and I'm pulling down sweat off this beer bottle. They gave me some tryouts to do commercials. Let me show you."

Abruptly, Charlie was out of his chair and down in a three-point football lineman's stance, facing Otis. "They took audition shots of me down like this, all in football gear, all made up by a big-tit blonde to look muddy and tired and bleeding, and then a voice on the commercial said, 'Hip one, hip two, hip three, hut!' Then I came right at the camera like I was going to hit somebody."

Charlie came right at Otis as if he were going to hit somebody—somebody named Otis.

Otis had a split second to imagine his body crushed, his soul crying out in pain. But Charlie stopped under a yard away and said off to his left, "I'd stop and straighten up and look right at the TV camera, take off my helmet, hold out my hand like this, and come back with a beer in it. And I'd say, 'When you work hard for a living, you need to have a way to relax after a hard day on the job. I'm Church Key Charlie Blue, and I'm sure the best way to relax is with an ice-cold Great America beer.' "

Otis wasn't sure what to do, so he applauded this old football player's commercial audition routine.

Said Charlie, "Thanks. Yeah, as you just saw, I was good. Damned good. But not good enough for the creeps running everything. They also told me—you know, like, 'by the way'— that my reputation for drinking beer might not work with the family-TV crowd. That gave me the name Church Key. They gave it to me in college. They said nobody could put down more beer than Church Key Charlie Blue. That was the goddamn truth then, and it still is. Great life, great country, ain't it? Great America. You got that church key I gave ya?"

Otis pulled it out of his pocket. "You bet," he said.

"Read what's engraved on it."

Otis leaned to his right and held the church key under the light of the floor lamp, which seemed, along with most everything else in the room, on the verge of collapsing.

There was the familiar bald-eagle logo of Great America beer, and under it, in small script, COMPLIMENTS OF CHURCH KEY CHARLIE BLUE.

Before Otis could say anything, Charlie said, "Instead of doing their commercials, Great America hired me to go around to bars on Monday nights—you know, during Monday Night Football—and hustle business for them. I had just retired from the Cowboys—retired 'cause they said I couldn't run anymore, the humpers—so I only went to places in Texas. East Texas, mostly, where the real rednecks live. I'd give out those church keys and do some autographing and a lot of grab-assing. The agent I had said it was public relations, and if I did it well, I would get another shot at commercials or move on to endorsing shoes and footballs and shit like that. I never moved on to nothing. Once you didn't need a church key to open a can of beer much anymore, they didn't need me to go around handing out church keys anymore either."

Otis considered the possibility of some MBA candidate at KU or Harvard or a similar place doing a case study on how the invention of the flip-top impacted the manufacture and sale and distribution of church keys in America.

"Did you always want to be a pro football player?" he asked Charlie.

Charlie, as if blowing up a balloon, raised his chest. "Since I first saw myself in the mirror."

"When was that?"

"When I was about two days old."

"College. Where did you go to college?"

"Little dipshit place in Oklahoma you never heard of." Charlie turned the sound back up and sat himself back down. Otis took a sip of his beer and remained still and silent as Charlie watched and listened while the Steelers kicked off to the Raiders to start the second half.

After a while, Otis's eyelids felt heavy. Running away from home in the rain had worn him out, and the beer had had an effect, and so had the lulling sound of voices and cheers. He set his beer bottle down on the floor.

As he did so, he noticed that Charlie also no longer had a beer in his hands; his eyes were closed, and his chin was resting heavily on his chest. Above the sounds of the television he honked out some of the loudest snoring Otis had ever heard. He was sure it could be picked up by travelers all along old U.S. 56, even through the rain.

Ignoring the fact that his clothes were wet and his shoes were muddy and even where he was or what in the hell was going on, Otis stretched out on the couch.

Soon he was also snoring loud enough for travelers to hear all along old U.S. 56.

SIX

O TIS WOKE UP to a jolt of strong, sweet odors—none of which he immediately recognized—and into a world of absolute confusion.

Those first few seconds after he opened his eyes were terrifying. *Where am I? What time is it? What is that smell? Why are my clothes so wet? Am I going to be late to work? Where is Sally?*

Is Pete Wetmore really dead?

Where is my Cushman?

Where in the hell is there a bathroom?

He sat straight up and looked around him. *The loony football player? Where is he? The giant? Was his name really Church Key Charlie Something?*

Where in the hell is he?

What is *that smell? It's like the one last night, only ten times stronger.*

What in the hell have I done?

Otis swung his feet around to the floor and stood up. There was the Cushman over by the door. Good.

In the cold light of early morning, the home of the monstrous man named after a beer can opener was more dirty, more messy, more everything crummy. Otis remembered a marine captain assigned to his naval ROTC unit at KU who, during inspections, called most everything he saw a "rat's nest." This place gave new and real meaning to that term.

Otis heard the sound of metal scraping from the concrete-block building next door. He began walking tentatively toward a wide-open door.

In the other building, standing over what appeared to be a huge hot stove, was Charlie. Blue? Charlie Blue. *Is his last name Blue?* Otis thought. He was wearing his Dallas Cowboys helmet and a pair of white latex gloves, the kind doctors and other health people use. In his right hand was a long wooden spoon that he was moving around in a huge cauldron-sized metal pot. There was steam flowing from the pot. And there was also that sweet smell.

Otis recognized the odor. It was chocolate. Heavy, grand, magnificent, glorious chocolate. It reminded him of fabulous Sunday afternoons at his grandmother's house in Medicine Lodge, southwest of Wichita. She had made fudge that, to Otis's taste, was the best in the world. The only downside was that she would never let Otis have as much as he wanted. "It'll make you sick, Otis," she'd say.

What in the hell is this? thought Otis.

"Good morning," he said to Charlie.

The monstrous man didn't even give Otis a glance. He said, "My crapper's on the disabled list. If you need to take a leak, just go out back to the woods and do it. I never lock the back door. Anything heavier, go over to the Gulf station just up the road to the right. Tell Johnny Gillette you're a friend of Church Key's, and he'll give you his crapper key. He's always up early."

"What are you making there?" Otis asked.

"Fudge."

Fudge. This loony, monstrous old three-time pro bowl football player is making fudge? That filth I saw on the man's body last night wasn't grease or oil—it was chocolate! This is crazy, this is absolutely crazy. Come see this, *Tonganoxie!* Otis thought.

Otis remembered *Charlie and the Chocolate Factory,* the fabulous children's book that he had read aloud to his daughter, Annabel. And wasn't there a movie later?

Willy Wonka would not have been caught dead in this chocolate factory. Church Key Charlie Blue's factory was as big a mess as his house. There was the stove in the center of the room, there was another ancient Kelvinator against a wall, and there were several waist-high tables scattered around. Many were covered with metal baking sheets full of what apparently were layers of poured fudge or top-tied plastic bags of fudge squares. The stove and the sheets and the tables were splattered with what appeared to be burnt chocolate. The floors were littered with empty bottles of vanilla and bags of sugar and brown Hershey's cocoa cans. The walls were covered with poorly framed photos and posters of football players. Otis assumed all of the players were Church Key in various stages and uniforms of his life, but there was no way to tell for sure, because the faces were obscured by helmets and face masks or distorted by wild grimaces or grins.

Otis decided he would go to the Gulf station and said so to Charlie, who made no vocal or physical response. He was clearly too occupied making fudge to care where Otis went.

It was a gorgeous, crisp morning. The sun was just above the horizon, on its way to being bright and full. The sky was clear and on its way to being that gorgeous blue it can be only on April days in Kansas. The rain was long gone, having left behind a few small puddles in the potholes and crevices of the driveway and roadway. Otis considered going by the Cushman and taking his toiletries with him to the Gulf station's crapper, but it seemed like an inappropriate thing to do. Shaving and brushing teeth were not crucial parts of Church Key Charlie's world. Otis felt the same way about changing into some of the dry clothes he had packed in the rear compartment of the Cushman. It also seemed natural and appropriate to remain in the damp clothes.

So. He had run away to this. And how far had he run? He figured it was twenty miles, at most, back east on old U.S. 56 to Eureka and to his home and office and life. But it seemed so much farther.

And he felt wonderful. It was crazy. Insane? But he felt great walking down this old road to use the bathroom at a Gulf station run by somebody named Johnny Gillette.

He wondered what time it was. He had asked himself a lot of questions since had he woken up on the raunchy red couch, but not that one. Now he looked at his wristwatch, a fifteen-hundred-dollar Omega that Sally had given him for Christmas two years ago.

It was 7:17.

A Monday morning at 7:17. If he were still at his home in NorthPark as Otis Halstead, insurance company CEO, civic leader, and devoted husband and father, he would at this moment be finishing breakfast. Probably a bowl of oatmeal and some fruit—blueberries, most likely. A cup of half-and-half coffee—half decaffeinated, half real. He would have already read the papers—*The Eureka Times* and *The Kansas City Star*—while riding his Exercycle, and he would have shaved, showered, and dressed in a dark suit, white shirt, and conservative tie. It was his uniform of work as much as those worn by police officers and bus drivers—and professional football tight ends.

In thirteen minutes, at seven-thirty, Otis Halstead, CEO, etc., would take off in his Explorer for downtown and the KCF&C Building, where he would begin his workday with a quick meeting at eight with senior staff. How are sales in Omaha/Lincoln? Any word on the planned Hallmark project in Kansas City? What's the outlook for our stock on the AMEX today?

He wondered how Sally had handled the notifications. He had left her a note on the small table in the kitchen, where she was sure to find it when she returned from church. It said:

My dearest,
By the time you read this, I will be gone. Where have I gone? I am not sure at this point. All I know is that the urge to leave, to run far, far away, is in me and it will not go away until I test it. I have gone on the motor scooter. I am perfectly all right, mentally and physically. The desire for a new and completely different life is quite normal. Please do not take this personally or see it in any way as a rejection of you. I love you very much. This has to do only with me. I have lived my life the way I was expected to, I have excelled the way I was expected to, I have accomplished what I was expected to. But something is missing. I do not know exactly what it is, but I know I must go now and try to find it. I know that if I do not try now that I will be miserable and make everyone around me—you the most—miserable, too.

Please pass on the news of my sudden departure and my regrets to Jack Thayer and the others at KCF&C. Tell them anything you wish, but my suggestion would be to keep it brief and nonspecific. Tell them only that I have suffered a harmless breakdown or disorder of some kind that makes it

impossible for me to continue to do my job for them. Bob
Gidney can probably be helpful in working out an
explanation. Somebody at Ashland will have an explanation
that will make it seem perfectly normal. Tell everyone at
the company that they should treat my absence the same
way they are treating Pete Wetmore's—as if I have died.
Whatever happens, I am relatively sure that running an
insurance company is not in my future.

This may not be a goodbye-forever to you, however. I
don't know yet. I hope I can make you understand that I
truly had no real choice but to do this.

Please do not attempt to find me. Please trust me when I
say that I am not mentally disturbed or ill. This is about the
soul, not the mind.

I took $5,000 from our savings account. Everything else
is yours.

I really do love you,
Otis

The Gulf station was no longer a Gulf station. It had been one
in an earlier life; some of the faded porcelain Good Gulf and other
signs were still around. But now, according to a roughly painted
red, white, and blue sign hanging out front, it was JOHNNY'S CAR
AND TRUCK REPAIR—FREE ESTIMATES—CASH AND CHECKS ONLY.
Clearly, Johnny Gillette and Charlie Blue ran their respective
businesses with the same consumer finance philosophy.

Otis heard a radio and some banging behind the small tat-
tered building. There, working on something under the hood of
a dark green 1987 Chevy pickup, was Johnny Gillette. He was
a black man about half the size of Charlie Blue and fifteen years
older.

Otis said he was a friend of Charlie Blue's, and could he use his restroom?

"You're lying," said Johnny Gillette. "Church Key ain't got no friends."

Otis wasn't sure if the other man was joking—putting him on. But the words were not accompanied by a smile.

"Well, he said to say that. I'm sorry," Otis said.

"I'm sure he did. I'm just saying it's a lie, that's all. The last friend Charlie had will be his first. Do you know him?"

Otis said he really didn't. Just met him, in fact.

"Had any of his fudge?"

"Not yet," Otis said. "Looking forward to it—a lot of it."

Johnny Gillette said, "Don't you think there's something weird about a grown man making bags and bags of chocolate fudge?"

Otis said yeah, it was pretty weird, all right.

"He's weird in a lot of ways, so watch yourself," said Johnny Gillette as he reached into his right-front pants pocket, pulled out a key, and handed it to Otis. "Leave it the way you found it, is all I ask. Okay?"

Otis promised to do that. Then he asked, "Did you always want to be a mechanic?"

"When I was a kid, I just wanted to grow up to be the boss, I didn't care what I was doing," said Johnny Gillette. "And you saw that sign out there, didn't ya?"

Otis followed Johnny Gillette's directions to the restroom inside the shop. It was remarkably clean and well equipped with toilet paper, paper towels, soap, and all of the essentials. It even smelled good, like soap.

As he did what he came to do, Otis thought about what Gillette had said about Church Key Charlie Blue not having any friends.

The thought made him sad for the monstrous fudge-making ex–football player back down the road.

But then he thought again and realized that someone could say the same thing about him—soon-to-be-sixty-year-old Otis Halstead—not having any *real* friends.

Maybe now, in this new life, he would have some.

OTIS FELT LIKE changing clothes. So instead of returning directly to the chocolate factory, Otis went first to Charlie Blue's house next door. The Red Ryder BB gun remained at the ready, hanging on the Cushman. He opened the scooter's rear storage compartment. There were the toy fire engine and the maps on top of the valise. Things seem to have shifted around from the travel and turmoil of yesterday, but at a glance, everything seemed present and accounted for.

He stripped down and dressed in all-clean, all-dry every-thing—from skivvies and socks to trousers and shirt. He laid the clothes he had taken off across the handlebars and seat of the scooter so they could dry.

He felt great. It didn't make sense. But he did.

He reentered Church Key Charlie Blue's world of chocolate.

"Make yourself useful, Oat-tus," said Charlie. "Put on a pair of these gloves—the health department will lock me up if you don't. They're the same as what the doctors put on to stick their finger up your ass to check your prostate. How many physicals have you had in your life, Oat-tus?"

Otis said he had not kept a good count.

Charlie said, "Well, I've had one million, four hundred thousand and twelve. Or more, even. They gave us one every three minutes, it seemed, when I was playing ball. Somebody was always poking on me or in me or up me somewhere."

Otis grabbed a pair of the gloves from a small box on the floor by the stove.

Charlie said, "Now cut those sheets of fudge into two-inch squares, then scoop 'em up one at a time with that spatula and put 'em in those plastic bags over there. Twelve—an even dozen—in each bag. There's a twist tie for each bag. Got it?"

Otis got it. He went immediately to work, using a chocolate-splattered wooden ruler to measure and then a chocolate-splattered carving knife to mark and cut through the scrumptious-looking sheets of fudge.

He filled two bags and moved on to the next table of uncut fudge as Charlie kept making more.

"Are you using a special recipe?" Otis, measuring and cutting and bagging, asked Charlie.

"I used to help Aunt Ninnie make it when I was a kid—the only thing I learned to do besides football—and I helped her sell it around town," Charlie said, not looking up from his work. "It's Hershey's powdered cocoa, sugar, butter, good milk, vanilla. Cook to a boil, test till it rolls good to a ball, and pour it out. It's the best there is. Take a piece, see for yourself."

Otis took a piece, ate it in two bites, and saw for himself. It was the most magnificent chocolate fudge he had ever had in his mouth. As good as—slightly better than, even—his grand-mother's.

"Spectacular," he said.

"Keep working, Oat-tus," said Charlie. "My morning cus-tomers'll be coming soon."

Oat-tus kept working, but he also kept eating. Piece after piece, piece after piece.

Finally, he got to eat as many as he wanted.

In a few minutes, people of various ages and fashions started coming through the door. Most carried large shopping bags or cardboard boxes. Each handed Charlie cash in exchange for bags of fudge, the exact number carefully counted out into the individual's respective container.

Within an amazingly fast half hour, all of the fudge was gone, and Charlie had a stack of paper money.

"Who were all those people?" Otis asked when it was over.

"They run or work for cafés and sweets shops and little grocery places around here," Charlie said. "Some of them take my fudge, claim they made it themselves, and mark up the price a bit. I do three batches a day—early morning, around noon, late afternoon."

Otis looked at the money Charlie had in his right hand, still gloved in plastic. "Looks like you did all right this morning," he said.

Charlie flipped his left hand through the bills as if he were a bank teller or a Las Vegas blackjack dealer. "Most of these are little things—there's probably not more than a hundred bucks here." He set the money down and reached up and took off his Dallas Cowboys helmet. "There's a lot more in here. Got it?"

Otis didn't get it.

Charlie turned the helmet upside down, stuck his right hand inside, and pulled out from behind the webbing a much larger stack of bills, held together by a large tan rubber band.

Otis recognized that rubber band.

"While you were over at Johnny Gillette's, I decided to check out you and your Cushman," said Charlie. "I found all of that money of yours, and I decided to split it with you."

Otis said nothing.

Charlie said, "I decided to split it four to one. Four thou for me, one thou for you. I left your thou in the case, so why don't you take your thou and your Cushman and get your butt on to running away."

"That makes you a thief," Otis said.

"Well, call a cop, then. Yeah, call a cop. Or sue me, scooter man. My guess is that there's no way you're going to do a damn thing. People carrying a lot of cash like this—particularly in neat stacks—are usually dealing drugs or doing something they aren't particularly proud of. I know, 'cause I've been there. That's why I'm here making fudge instead of running loose back in Texas right now. Probation. Got to keep my nose clean, save some money—including some of yours, Oat-tus—to make some restitutions and pay some fines. But you ain't calling no cops down on me and my probation. The only thing you can do is get your butt on down the road before I decide to take your thou, too."

Otis considered his options. He could think of only one: Retreat and get out of here. And leave with only the silent satisfaction—and rationalization—that this stupid football player may have taken four thousand dollars, but he'd left an antique toy fire truck worth three times that.

Otis couldn't leave without leaving behind a few words. "Johnny Gillette said you had no friends, and I can certainly understand why. I come back here and help you do your work and be friendly. I don't have any friends, either. I was thinking you're a man trying to work hard to make a living, and what is it you really are? You're a goddamn thief. No wonder you don't have any friends, and at the rate you're going, you'll never have any."

"At the rate I'm going, it's too late for me to have a friend," Charlie said. "Get your butt gone, scooter man."

Within minutes, Otis put on his Chiefs helmet, stuffed his damp clothes into the back of the scooter with his other things, and rolled the scooter outside. He hoped that being inside overnight had dried out the Pacemaker's little engine.

Otis assumed Charlie was watching him from a window in the factory side. He kicked down on the starter. It turned over, but no fire. He twisted the throttle farther and kicked it harder. The motor sputtered.

Then it popped. And sputtered again. This time it caught.

Otis mounted, gunned it, released the brake, and took off west once again on old U.S. 56.

He was furious with himself as much as he was with this stupid idiot football player. *He steals my money, and what does Otis the new man do? He makes a speech,* Otis thought.

Otis figured he was the same as the quarterback on TV whom Charlie had yelled at to throw it out of bounds.

SEVEN

OTIS HADN'T BEEN back on the road ten minutes when
he needed to have a cup of coffee. And maybe something
unsweet to eat. The great fudge of that thieving Church Key
football has-been had left Otis with a slight twinge of nausea in
his throat. Yes, his grandmother had been right about eating too
much fudge.

He started looking for somewhere to stop.

There was a boarded-up place that once was what appeared to
have been a fairly elegant steak house. There were the long-
closed coffee shops of two deserted motels and the remains of
what must have once been a busy truck stop and café.

Kansas was well known for its deserted places, its thousands—
six thousand, at least, according to the Kansas State Historical
Society—of dead towns born of people's dreams that didn't come
true. Otis knew, from his tenure as vice president of the society,
that most of them had been created in the late 1800s by enter-
prising immigrants from the East or Europe. Some came to get
rich by erecting factories—cement factories were a particular
favorite—or mining for coal, lead, zinc, and other Kansas natural
resources. Others came to be free and happy by transforming
pieces of open Kansas land into individual visions of paradise.

There were socialist communes, hot-springs resorts, camps for buffalo-hunting safaris, pro-slavery/anti-slavery fortresses for whites and blacks-only havens for escaped/freed slaves, a Presbyterian town, a Jewish agricultural colony, a community of fancy young Englishmen who substituted coyotes for foxes in their to-the-hounds hunts, a vegetarian settlement laid out in accordance with an octagonal plan. Several of these ghostly spots were on or near old Highway 56, including one not too much farther west, where a wealthy Frenchman had come in 1870 with the families of forty expert silkworm farmers to establish the new silk capital of the world.

Otis, his desire for coffee growing, was about to consider a detour over to the interstate when, finally, up ahead he saw a small vertical flashing sign. MARY BETH'S, it said in foot-high letters, with EATS crossing near the top like a T.

He pulled off the road and saw immediately that Mary Beth's was to cafés what Church Key Charlie Blue's was to factories and Johnny Gillette's was to vehicle repair shops. It was a very small, very old art deco stucco building that was suffering mightily from age and neglect and deterioration. Years ago it may very well have been a snazzy little diner-type place.

Now he saw huge cracks and holes in the stucco, which had begun, no doubt, as pure white but was now a musty, rusty, sandy color. Inside, there was a counter with a few stools and six or seven booths covered with split and chipped red vinyl. The black-and-white tile floor was also split and chipped.

But the place was open for business. At this moment that was all that concerned Otis.

There were two men sitting at the counter and two other men sitting across from each other at one of the booths. No one was talking, and there was no music playing. The only sound was from the crackling of grease somewhere in back behind the counter. Something was being fried. Otis couldn't tell from the smell what it was. Bacon, maybe. Or sausage. Hash browns? An egg over easy?

Something on the counter immediately caught his eye. There was one of Church Key Charlie Blue's bags of fudge. A hand-lettered sign leaning against it said: HOMEMADE FRESH TODAY— 50 CENTS APIECE. Otis resisted the urge to grab them and toss them out and away as far as he could.

"Mary Beth!" one of the men at the counter yelled. "You've got a customer in need out here!"

Otis smiled down at the man, who was in his sixties, very tanned in the face and around the neck, and dressed like a farmer. "Thank you, sir," Otis said quietly, respectfully.

"Service isn't what they do here," said the man. He said it in a friendly manner.

And there in front of Otis stood somebody who had to be Mary Beth. She was much older than her restaurant, seventy, at least, tiny, and very gray—both her hair and her shriveled, tired skin.

"I'm so sorry, but I'm out of everything but toast, bacon, eggs, and coffee this morning," she said with a weariness that was stunning, scary. She seemed about to drop—dead, maybe— right there before everybody. "Fudge—I've got some fudge there, too, as you can see. Not the right thing to eat for break-fast, though, is it? You look familiar. Didn't I see you at that crazy football player's this morning?"

Otis only smiled. He was not anxious to confirm that he'd had anything to do with the thieving idiot called Church Key. But there was nothing he could do about it now. He told Mary Beth he'd love two pieces each of toast and bacon.

"Help yourself to a cup of coffee from the pot over there, and have a seat anywhere," she said.

Otis chose a booth two down from the one that was occupied.

One of the two men in it yelled amiably at Otis, "We were just talking about Joe Montana. Was he as good as Len Dawson? I saw your Chiefs helmet there. What do you think?"

Montana and Dawson had played quarterback for the Kansas City Chiefs at different times. Otis had seen them play in person at Arrowhead Stadium in Kansas City and on television.

"I'd say they were about the same," Otis said. "Both were great."

"Yeah," said the man. "That helmet looks like the real McCoy. Charlie Blue got his real one from the Cowboys. Did you see it?"

"I did. This one's real, too. I bought it at a sporting goods store."

"Why?" said the other man. He and his companion were wearing blue work clothes. Otis recognized the logos over their left breasts as being that of the CKP&L—Central Kansas Power and Light.

"I bought it for my son, and he loans it to me when I ride the scooter," Otis lied.

The two men had clearly watched him arrive on the Cushman, which Otis could see from his place in the booth. They had probably been talking about the old unshaved guy who just drove up on an old motor scooter wearing a Chiefs helmet.

"Is that a twenty-two hanging off the scooter?" one of the men asked.

"It's an air rifle," Otis replied and, anticipating a follow-up, added, "I use it to shoot rats and cats and gnats."

The two men from CKP&L looked at each other and said no more.

Otis went back to feeling really good about himself.

He checked his watch again. It was 10:35 A.M. He tried to imagine what was happening now at his old offices in Eureka. Who, if anyone, was crying over the disappearance of the CEO; who, if anyone, was reading the boring goddamn reports he would be reading, and running the boring goddamn meetings instead of him? He worried for a few hard minutes—it was the first time it had crossed his mind—about the stockholders of Kansas Central Fire and Casualty. The stock had been selling on the AMEX at thirty-four a share on Friday when the market closed. Once the word was out on his disappearance this morning, it might take a hit of three or four points. The running away of a company's CEO can do that to a stock. But if the institutional types—pensions and mutual funds—didn't panic, everything would settle down in a few days. Jack Thayer would figure out a way to signal stability to stockbrokers and stockholders and policyholders and employees and the world. KCF&C would be fine without Otis Halstead. He had never thought so before, but sitting here now in this booth at Mary Beth's on old U.S. 56 west of Eureka, he was sure of it.

Speaking of Mary Beth, he noticed that she was talking to somebody. She was speaking loudly, and so was the other person—a man.

Otis turned toward the noise.

"I gave you a twenty, Mary Beth, goddammit," said the farmer who had summoned her on Otis's behalf a few minutes before. He was standing at the end of the counter with the cash register between him and Mary Beth.

"Don't you goddamn me, Duane Williamson," she said. "You know what it does to my arthritis."

"There's no connection between cussing and arthritis," said the man. "You're trying to steal my money again, and playing sick isn't going to change it one whit."

Otis may have imagined it, but it seemed as if Mary Beth's face went from concrete-block gray to blazing red in a split second. "You gave me a ten! Now, you take your change and your cheating self out of here and out of my sight before I call the sheriff and have you arrested for disturbing the peace and making a slander against me."

"I ain't going nowhere without ten more bucks, and that's it."

"Then you're going to jail or your grave."

The customer stepped around the corner and moved his right hand toward the cash register drawer. Mary Beth slammed it shut on some of his fingers, and he screamed.

"You old thief!" he yelled at her. "One day you and this place are going to burn like you're in hell itself!"

Otis stood up and started moving toward them. He remembered reading a story in *The Kansas City Star* a few years ago about an incident over ten dollars in change at a Dairy Queen in some East Texas town. It was between some cowboy kid and a waitress, and before it was over, there was a live TV standoff, gunplay, and at least one person dead—maybe both the waitress and the customer.

Otis wasn't going to let that happen here. Maybe he hadn't reacted the way he should have to save Pete Wetmore's life. Whatever, he sure as hell was not going to make that mistake again.

He approached them with a ten-dollar bill in his hand. "Here," he said to the man. "Take this, and that'll end it."

"What business is it of yours?" said the man.

"Just trying to keep the peace, that's all. And that's worth ten bucks any day, anytime."

"I don't want your money," the guy said and stalked out the front door.

Mary Beth disappeared through a swinging door that Otis assumed was to the kitchen.

Otis turned to go back to his booth. The other three customers in the place—the two from CKP&L and the second man at the counter—were still sitting, and they were smiling at him.

"Why didn't you all try to help out?" he asked the three in a kind of joint accusation. "Somebody could have gotten hurt—killed, even."

"No way," said the man at the counter. "They're both Williamsons—second cousins or something. They fight over something every morning."

Before too long, Otis was back on old U.S. 56, having left a twenty-dollar bill under the corner of his empty plate.

His throat was completely fudge-nausea-free after he'd eaten two pieces of fairly brown wheat toast and two pieces of crisp bacon and drunk two cups of coffee. The sweetness was gone, but the Church Key Charlie Blue fury was still stuck way back up in there.

SOON HE WAS on the western outskirts of Marionville, Kansas, famous for being the birthplace of more Congressional Medal of Honor winners per capita than any city or town in America (seven out of a population of twenty-five hundred) and as the birthplace of Larry Winston Weir, the inventor of rippled potato chips. Both distinctions were commemorated with small sections in the city-county historical society's museum on the square. Otis knew that because he had gone there on the historical society's VIP bus tour of central Kansas's historical sites.

This trip to Marionville was as a VIP runaway on a motor scooter.

He remembered that earlier tour mostly for the stops at a few of the twenty-four round barns that had been built in the early 1900s and remained in various stages of use and restoration throughout Kansas. There was one just west of Marionville, if he recalled correctly, that was particularly stunning. It was a concrete and wood structure that was sixty feet in diameter and seventy-five feet tall in its domed center. From a distance, it looked like a strange, out-of-place castle in the middle of the prairie.

Marionville was also known for its brick streets, most of them having been laid years ago, during the peak of the town's prosperity from a nearby air force base. The bricks were famous Coffeyville bricks, manufactured in the southeast Kansas town of Coffeyville. But prosperity had disappeared from Marionville, and with it had gone the town's ability to properly maintain the remaining bricks and replace those that were broken or missing. The end result was a street system that was mostly an obstacle course that rattled bones and teeth, dislodged hubcaps, and blew out tires.

Otis, realizing the peril, throttled his scooter down to a slow creep as he entered the town and kept his eyes hard on the roadway, looking for dangerous holes and bumps. The road made a series of sharp turns before it straightened out to go through downtown and by the square. He made it fine until he came almost to the end of the brick on the west side of town, where old U.S. 56 switched from brick back to cracked and neglected concrete.

He relaxed and took his eyes off the road in front of him and began observing the sights and scenery again. On his right was the once-proud WELCOME, HIGH FLIERS gate to the once-proud Galva Air Force Base, one of several facilities in Kansas built during World War II to train B-29 bomber crews. It had remained active as a training base during the Korean War and for a while as some kind of intelligence facility during Vietnam. Now it was deserted, its runways grown over with grass, its fences covered with vines, its stories and the people who lived them—

Suddenly, Otis was flying through the air.

He landed on his head, the Chiefs helmet whamming hard against the highway. He was conscious but hurting. He heard the screeching of brakes and turned over and looked up to see the blur of a blue pickup truck coming right at him. He rolled to his left, and the truck jerked to the right, its left front tire brushing slightly against the helmet and Otis.

Otis moved his legs to stand up. They worked. He stretched his arms. They worked. He removed his helmet. His head didn't come off inside it. He could see and smell. And there was no blood.

The helmet had a harsh scrape across its top and right side. His $185 Kansas City Chiefs helmet had saved his life.

"Are you all right, sir?" said a young male voice.

Otis turned in its direction and saw a kid in his late teens, tall, blond, crew-cut. He was rolling the Cushman toward Otis.

Otis noticed that they were in the middle of the road, and a few cars had stopped in both directions. There was no huge backup. It would have taken days of stalled traffic to create a huge backup on old U.S. 56.

"I'm fine," Otis said to the young man.

"You want an ambulance?"

"No, no. No need for that. I'm still all in one piece."

"Then let's move off the highway."

Otis followed the young man and the Cushman to the high-way shoulder, where the pickup—Otis recognized it as a Dodge Ram—had come to rest.

The kid waved the cars in both directions to go about their business, and Otis's brush with death was over. As best as he could tell, the scrapes to his wonderful lifesaving helmet and right knee and leg were all the damage that had been done.

The kid said, "Thank God that scooter of yours and that Chiefs helmet coming toward me grabbed my full attention— so I was looking when you took your fall and could react in time to keep from running right over you."

Yes, thought Otis. *Thank God and you, young man.*

Otis inspected his 1952 Pacemaker. It looked no worse for wear than he did. "I must have hit a hole in the road," he said.

"That's mostly all there is in this old highway," said the kid. "Can I take you somewhere?"

Otis really liked this young man. "What's your name?" he asked.

"Tom Caldwell. T is what everybody calls me—because there are a lot of Toms in my family," said the kid. "It's a plain T without the period. My parents said if an S without a period was all right for Harry S Truman, then that was fine for their son." He extended his right hand.

Otis took it and said, "I'm Buck."

"Nice to meet you, Buck," said T Caldwell. "Where are you headed, anyhow?"

"West—to Salina and beyond."

T Caldwell said, "I live just around the corner. I had run out to get some magazines for my mom. Want to come by for a cup of coffee or something?"

Buck said he would love to.

THE CALDWELL HOUSE was a one-story freshly painted white frame with green shutters, a shingle roof, and a clean trimmed yard and flower garden in front. This kind of house in this kind of neighborhood was right out of Otis's life in Sedgwicktown. As he scootered up to the house behind T's truck, he realized that it was all still pretty much the same. Eureka was larger, and the houses—those in NorthPark in particular—were larger and newer, but most everything else was about the same.

About the same. Maybe that was the story of his life? About the same. Everything about him, Otis the Responsible, was always about the same as it had always been. Well, that was not exactly right. Hadn't his father's death changed him? What about being bald? Could that idiot Tonganoxie be right about that?

He was no longer Otis the Responsible. Now he was Buck.

"My mom is very sick with a bad liver disease, Buck," T said as they walked up the front sidewalk. "It's got a very long name—primary sclerosing cholangitis—and there's no cure. She doesn't get her hair fixed much anymore, so she doesn't like to see a lot of people."

Otis said he understood. He took off his football helmet and swept his right hand across his barren scalp. It marked the first pleasant thought and happy gesture he'd had about not having any hair. "Tell her I'm not big on fixed hair, either," he said.

T smiled and said, "Good for you, sir. Sometimes she puts on a Central State baseball cap that I gave her, but she says it makes her head itch like she's a puppy with fleas. Mostly, she sees only me and other family and old friends, anyhow."

Otis said he understood. But he really didn't. The only person really close to him who'd died was his father, and that had happened suddenly, violently, in an accident.

Inside, T went off to the left to see about his mother. He told Otis to make himself comfortable, pointing right, toward what was clearly the living room. The interior, like the exterior, was tidy, precise, immaculate. Otis looked around for photographs and other specific signs of this family's life, but before he found much of anything, T returned.

"She's put on the cap to see you, even though I told her you were bald and didn't care about hair," T said. "Mom says she's curious to see any strange man I brought home—particularly one who's riding around on an old motor scooter and one whose life I saved."

Otis had never been comfortable around really sick people. He had trouble looking at them without feeling embarrassed, ashamed that they were sick and he wasn't. He never knew what to say, and he often said too much or the wrong things. He had wanted to tell T that he didn't want to see his mother, but that would have been impossible.

"What kind of scooter is it?" asked Iola Caldwell after her son had introduced her and Otis. Her voice was cracked, high-pitched, but firm.

"It's a Cushman," Otis replied.

"That's what I figured."

Iola Caldwell was sitting up in bed, propped up by several pillows. Her head was mostly covered by a red baseball cap with CENTRAL in script across the front. Some thin strands of dark brown hair were showing on the sides. Her skin was yellow, like slick paper, but her blue eyes sparkled out at Otis. He could not tell how old she was but thought probably in her fifties. He could not tell what she had looked like before she got sick, but he figured probably very attractive. She made only a tiny lump under the bedcovers, but there was no way to know what her original size had been. Could she have been as large a woman as her son was a man?

There was something about her manner, her style, that did not make Otis want to turn away, to leave the room. He didn't mind looking at her, listening to her.

"T's father won me with a Cushman. He was the only boy in high school here in Marionville who had one. He offered to take me on a ride, and he took me forever—almost forever. I loved sitting there behind him with my arms around his waist. I was the envy of every girl. I mean, *every* girl."

Otis said, "Would you like to take a quick ride on mine?"

The blue eyes brightened like new stars. To her son, she said, "Take me out there, T."

"Mom, are you sure?" said T.

"I'm really sure."

Otis almost cried as he watched the son reach under his mother's frail, shrunken body and lift her up into his arms. Both were careful that her pink chenille robe covered her completely. Her feet were bare. Otis saw a pair of pink slippers on the floor by the side of the bed. In a completely natural move, he reached down, picked up the slippers, and stuck them one at a time on her feet.

"Onward, Buck," T said.

"Onward, Buck," his mother said.

Outside on the street, Otis sat down on the scooter first, with both feet on the ground. Then he felt the warmth of a small shaking body behind him and two thin arms around his stomach.

"Slowly, now, Buck," T said.

Otis smiled and pushed off the scooter with his right foot. It coasted a few feet, and he inched the throttle up a whisk. He was struck by her smell. It was a mixture of medicine and powder and soap, like that of a well-run hospital. He felt her head hard against his back and her hands hard against his stomach. But she didn't seem to be afraid. She had done this before; she had been on the back of a Cushman before. She was comfortable here.

A skinny old woman in a blue housecoat came out of the house next door. She waved her bony right hand at Iola and yelled in a surprisingly loud voice, "Look at you, look at you, look at you."

"Look at me is right, Grace," Iola Caldwell called back, but her words probably didn't carry all the way to Grace.

Otis drove the scooter as slowly as it would go without tipping over. He went down the road—a narrow, well-maintained blacktop—for about fifty yards and then made a swing around and came back.

"Are you okay?" he asked her as he made the swinging turn.

"Like being in heaven," she said.

Those were the only words they exchanged in the five minutes they shared on the 1952 Pacemaker.

As T lifted her off, she said to Otis, "What's that gun about?"

"It's a BB gun, Mom, not a real one," T said.

"I hate guns," she said. "I've never let T have even one of those."

Her son carried her back inside the house after she exchanged several hearty waves with Grace, who, smiling happily, had not left her front sidewalk. She had been a loyal audience.

Otis followed at a distance but, instead of going back into Iola's bedroom, stayed in the entrance hall. In a few minutes, T came back out.

"She enjoyed that," he said to Otis. "Thank you for doing it. Can I get you some coffee or iced tea or something?"

Otis truly did not know what to do. He very much wanted to stay here awhile in this house, with this young man and his dying mother. But it didn't make sense.

"She told me to tell you to shave," T said. "She said a grown man like you shouldn't go around looking the way you do. I told her I'd tell you, and I did."

But she doesn't understand, thought Otis. *I am running away from home. Grown men who run away from home do not shave. They also do not brush their teeth.*

Otis knew T expected some explanation, some real story about how and why he was out there on old Highway 56 on an antique motor scooter. No stories. Otis changed the subject. "What's your situation, T?" he asked.

T hesitated for a second but then answered, "I'm a junior at Central State, but I took this semester off to be here at home with Mom. Her liver disease, just so you know, isn't caused by drinking or anything like that. Nobody knows where it comes from. It just comes. She ought to have a transplant, but her heart's not up to it, which goes back to some problem she had when she was a kid. I don't get it. She's only forty-six years old. But what it means is that she doesn't have much longer, so I figured it was more important to be here with her than to be at school. I can finish that later . . . you know, afterward."

Yes, Otis knew what "afterward" meant. His mother had died at the age of seventy-one, twelve years ago, from complications caused by a badly done gallbladder operation. He said to T, "It must be so difficult taking care of her. I admire you for doing it."

"There's a hospice nurse who comes in the house every day when I'm not here. The worst part, frankly, is taking Mom to the bathroom. I have to stay in there with her so she doesn't slip or fall. She hates it that I'm in there as much as I do."

Otis had nothing to say. He couldn't imagine ever being in the bathroom with his own mother while she . . . well, went to the bathroom. There had never been much of a personal nature between him and his mother, who was a shy woman overshadowed, even in Otis's memory, by her husband almost to irrelevance.

Otis started walking back toward the front door. He was going to leave T and Iola Caldwell and their white frame house in Marionville, Kansas.

He asked after a few seconds, "Where's your dad? The man who gave her her first Cushman ride?"

"He and Mom divorced several years ago. He lives in California, but he sends us money for her, and for me to go to school. He's a criminal lawyer, and one of the reasons Mom's so hot against guns is because he helps criminals with guns stay out of jail. That's what she says, at least."

Otis wanted to know more. He wanted to know why Iola Caldwell and her husband divorced. He wanted to know everything about this family, these people, their life.

They were out on the sidewalk now. He thought he'd try one more question. "What kind of relationship do you have with your father?"

"I hate the son of a bitch. As far as I'm concerned, I don't have a father."

Buck will be your father! Otis wanted to yell. But he remained silent.

T said, "He ran off with his partner's secretary. She was pretty and young and sexy. I think it gave Mom her sickness."

"That doesn't cause liver disease, T."

T waved that statement off into the air. This son, this exceptional young man, knew damned well his father's screwing around had caused his mother's sickness. It was clear nobody would or could ever convince him otherwise.

Otis re-covered his bald scalp with the Chiefs helmet and mounted his scooter.

"That helmet makes you look a lot younger," said the exceptional young man.

"I know," said Otis. "Thanks again for saving my life, T."

"Anytime, Buck. Where exactly are you going?"

"Just west on old 56," Otis said. "That's all I know."

"The Chanute River Bridge is closed the other side of Dearing. There's a detour a couple of miles west of town. You'll have to leave 56 there for a while—fifteen miles or so."

Otis said, "What are you studying in college—what do you want to be?" One last question; the one Otis seemed to ask everyone these days.

"I have no idea, to tell you the truth. I'm just going to college and then go on away somewhere."

"You won't live here?"

"No, sir. My mom says there are some people who are meant to go and some who are meant to stay. She says I'm one of the goers, and I think she's right."

Otis wanted to ask T to come with him to beat up an old football player named Charlie Blue and take his money back, but he resisted the urge. Charlie could have handled both of them with one hand.

Instead, he shook the young man's hand and scootered away, back toward old U.S. 56.

Out of new habit, he remembered another of his states' jingles.

If I loved Carol of Raleigh,
And she hit a baseball out of sight,
I'd call it a long Carol-liner.

EIGHT

WHERE WAS THAT old round barn? At first he almost missed it, about a hundred yards off the highway on the right. He pulled off to see what he could see. There wasn't much left. Part of the dome was gone, and so were many of the shingles on the roof that swept up to it. There were also huge gaps in the wooden planking and even in the concrete base. The farmer who owned the barn had decided to let it go away, to disappear, to fall into nothing.

You idiot! Otis wanted to yell at the farmhouse nearby. He was no rabid preservationist, but his five years on the historical society board, which he had done mostly for civic duty, had left him with an appreciation for the simple good sense of preserving the special things of our history. Round barns were special.

So were the state's ghost towns, such as the Frenchman's silk town. Within a few minutes, there was the twelve-inch-square metal sign, SITE OF SILKTOWN. That poor Frenchman. He'd bought three thousand acres for his new town, promising to develop "a system of industrial and social life far in advance of either now prevailing in the world." The silk farming did flourish for a while, and so did a large cheese and butter business and a vast orchard of mulberry trees. The community boasted several mansions, including the Frenchman's, which had sixty rooms and was, for many years, the largest private dwelling in the state of Kansas. But after twenty years, then in his eighties, the Frenchman gave it all away to the Odd Fellows Lodge for an orphanage and returned to France. All that remained was this small historical marker and the ruins of a deserted school.

Otis could see the white stone remnants of the old schoolhouse in the trees behind a fence on another farmer's private property. Otis slowed down but did not stop or even think about yelling at this farmer, a man named Troy Mulberry, who had tried—without success—to preserve what was left of the Frenchman's dream.

Soon Otis was moving again at full putt-putt speed, thinking about that Frenchman. What kind of special, courageous people were he and all of the others who came to this rough country of Kansas to begin new lives? Otis thought, *It's not the same thing, but what I'm doing right now on this Cushman is . . .* kind *of the same thing. Isn't it?*

In a few minutes, Otis could see the modest skyline of Dearing—silhouettes of a few new bank and old office buildings and several grain elevators. Dearing was a wheat town of eleven thousand or so people, known mostly for the Mennonite college that housed and supported some of the best Turkey Red wheat researchers and historians in America.

There were a few more cars and trucks on the road as he got closer to the city limits. With no warning, Otis was overcome with exhaustion. He thought for a second he might pass out or even disintegrate and die.

The scrapes and bruises from his spill had been temporarily masked by the exhilaration of being with T and Iola Caldwell. But now Otis's knee was burning, his bruised skin was aching, and he thought that at least two or three bones of various sizes and locations had been cracked. Most of his internal organs had been shaken up and out of place.

He saw from the horizon that it was late afternoon and from his watch that it was almost five o'clock.

He had to stop, to rest his weary and injured body and his equally spent and fatigued soul.

Then he saw the familiar blue, yellow, red, and white sign of a Best Western hotel. *Thank you, oh Lord of the hospitality industry,* he thought, *for concluding that the city of Dearing is large enough to support and important enough to rate a real motel.*

Within another ten minutes, he was in room 145, a first-floor nonsmoking room with a king-size bed. It took the last of his energy, but as a security precaution, he rolled the scooter inside the room and set it against the wall next to a radiator. Central Kansas was no hotbed of crime—the thievery of Church Key Charlie Blue being a rare exception—but there was also no need to tempt anyone with the easy theft of a priceless 1952 Cushman Pacemaker.

Without taking off anything except his shoes, he fell onto the bed. He couldn't remember a time when he'd been more spent, more used up. He closed his eyes to sleep, but what came instead were thoughts of where he was, what he was doing, and what he had already done. The escape, the rain, the fudge and thievery of Church Key Charlie Blue, Johnny Gillette, Mary Beth's café, the spill, T and his mother, Iola.

All of it had happened in just a day and a half, and he was still only about twenty miles from Eureka.

He thought about Russ Tonganoxie, the long-haired, chino-wearing idiot psychiatrist. *What, pray tell, would he be saying to me now?* Otis thought.

Halstead, you really are crazy.

Yes, I am definitely crazy. Just like you, Tonganoxie. Sniffles lead to

*a runny nose, which leads to a cold, which leads to pneumonia. Buying
an antique toy fire engine leads to a BB gun and a Kansas City Chiefs
helmet, which leads to a Cushman, which leads to insanity, which leads
to dreams of running away with a stranger half my age named Sharon
and then to really running away from home all alone.*

He thought about Kansas Central Fire and Casualty, his priv-
ileged life as a CEO. His salary of $250,000 a year, plus a year-
end bonus based on the company's performance. KCF&C always
did well, so he always did well at bonus time because it was cal-
culated as a percentage of his salary. Last year the bonus was
$50,000. In addition to the money, he had a terrific pension and
stock options program as well as the normal CEO perks of first-
class air travel and membership in two country clubs and
Eureka's top downtown private club.

But KCF&C and all that went with it were in an earlier life,
a life that was gone—and gone forever. The few KCF&C
thoughts he did have were mostly about what they would do
with his small handful of personal things. There were photographs of Sally and Annabel on the back credenza, and on the
walls hung his framed college diplomas and signed photographs
of him with Bob Dole and Nancy Kassebaum, the Eureka Man
of the Year plaque and the United Way leadership certificate,
and other remains of his life as a civic leader and leading citizen
of Eureka, Kansas. On his desk were a small gold clock that had
been presented to him after his year as president of Rotary, and
an engraved sterling silver pen-and-pencil set that he'd gotten
from the National Association of Insurance Executives for serv-
ing as its president. And there were his small specially printed
memo pads that had not only his name and title but also
stickum slivers at the top, like a Post-it.

None of these things mattered. There was only one object
that did. It was a magnificent thirty-six-by-twenty-four photo-

graph of several shaggy buffalo roaming the tall grass prairie near Council Grove. There was a light snow falling in the foreground and the hint of a late-season sunset in the background. A gifted Oklahoma photographer had taken the picture, which, even up close, resembled a painting as much as a photograph. To Otis, it was a piece of art. He had never thought of or appreciated photography as an art form until he saw that picture hanging in a gallery in Kansas City. He paid twelve hundred dollars for it, more than he had ever paid for anything like that, and he saw it as a tremendous bargain. Now he hoped somebody at the company had the good sense to give it to Sally or otherwise take care of it in his permanent absence. They could throw out all of the other so-called art on his walls, all the paintings of flowers and apples and similar inanimate objects.

What a nothing life he had led. And that buffalo picture said it all. It was the only thing he had to show for his fifty-nine years that was of any value to him. Except for the fire engine and the BB gun and the football helmet and the Cushman, all of which he had just acquired. What had he done with his fifty-nine, soon-to-be sixty, years? And his millions of seconds, thousands of minutes, hundreds of days and months?

Amen, Anthony Hopkins. I, too, have wasted my life. I, too, look back on my life and see a desert wasteland.

He thought of Sharon. He considered her face and hair and eyes and fully clothed body from the two times he had seen her. Then he considered, ever so slowly and delightfully, what she might look like nude, lying in the sunshine on that quilt alongside Farnsworth Creek, reading Beschloss. He removed her clothes, one small garment at a time, to see for sure. He was not surprised to discover that her young body was fresh and soft and shiny and slick and sweet. He ran both of his hands over her . . .

Then came an eruption of wet. Damn! Damn, damn. This is for little boys! But it came rushing and gushing all over his underwear and into his trousers and down his fifty-nine-year-old legs.

He was horrified. But the horror lasted for only a second or two. Then he laughed—and laughed and laughed. He had had a wet dream! He couldn't remember the last time he'd had one. Then he remembered when it was. Not as a little boy. It was one night after he had danced with Betsy McPherson at an office Christmas party. Betsy was an assistant vice president for finance who was neither particularly beautiful nor particularly sexy. There was just something about her, about the way she walked and sat and talked, that turned Otis on. He could not have explained it, and fortunately, he never had to, because he never made anything even remotely resembling a suggestive comment, much less a real pass, physical or otherwise. All that ever happened was that he went home that night after the party and, late at night in bed next to Sally, he had a wet dream.

Wet dreams were not from the lives of responsible men, not courageous men on quests for new lives. They were like Cushmans and Daisy Red Ryder air rifles and football helmets and cast-iron toy fire trucks.

He got out of bed, went to the bathroom, and cleaned himself up with a towel.

And he lay back down.

He didn't feel so exhausted. He didn't feel as if he were going to disintegrate. He didn't even feel he was crazy anymore. *Isn't it interesting what a wet dream about a young maiden named Sharon can do for an old man?* Otis thought. He figured Tonganoxie and the other shrinks at Ashland would have a field day—or professional wet dreams of their own, so to speak—with material like this.

There was a fairly good-sized television set—a twenty-one-inch or more screen—on a chest against the wall right in front of him. It was accompanied by a *TV Guide* and a remote control on the bedside table. He switched on the set and began surfing.

The news was on. The news wasn't what it used to be. Otis had not been able to figure out what had happened to the minds of the people who ran national television news. When there were Huntley-Brinkley and Walter Cronkite and Harry Reasoner and Eric Sevareid and John Chancellor, the reporting had seemed calm, straight, newsy, relevant, necessary to watch. Now it wasn't any of those things. He had read in *The Wall Street Journal* recently that the cable news networks hadn't been the same since the O. J. Simpson and Monica Lewinsky stories, and they, plus the Internet, had scared the commercial networks into trying to make their newscasts more like entertainment, more like what the cable people were doing with the news. It wasn't working, because the audiences already had plenty of other ways to be entertained. Such as the circus.

Otis seldom watched any news programs, not even the local ones, except when there was a major national or international news crisis or an area weather emergency. The local newscasts in Eureka were mostly about people screaming at one another or crying and dying violently. The rest were a few breathlessly delivered sports scores, elaborate weather forecasts, and inane chat and giggles among all of the on-air people involved.

He now surfed right through every newscast and news channel, looking for a movie or a British mystery or an A&E history documentary or something that might distract him for a while.

Nothing. He clicked it off.

It was quiet again in room 145. There was no highway noise from old U.S. 56, no noise at all. Now he had to think about himself again.

Okay, Otis, what now? Okay, Buck, *what now?*

Sleep. I will sleep now. I will close my eyes and dream not of Sharon nor of KCF&C. I will imagine a life somewhere farther west that—

What in the hell is this? I can't imagine a life different from the one I've lived, because it's the only one I know anything about. This is ridiculous!

He decided to think of something he had done or experienced or seen or felt in each of his fifty-nine years. One year at a time.

Nothing during year one, of course. Or year two. What about year three? Didn't I first smell cow shit in the barn when I was three? Also, Mom read me a book about a soldier who saved a cat from drowning at the front in France . . .

He reached for the phone and called his home number in Eureka.

Sally answered on the first ring. There was something in her voice that told him she had been answering the phone on the first ring since the moment she found out that her husband had run away.

"What is this about, Otis?" she said.

"I don't know."

"I thought I had lost you forever, Otis. Have I?"

"I think so, but I don't know."

"Is it about sex?"

Sally spoke quietly. Surprisingly so. There was no anger in her tone. He had expected some shouts, some noise, some commotion, some shit.

"Sex?"

"Sex."

"There's no woman with me, if that's what you mean."

"I don't know exactly what I mean, but that's a good beginning, something I'm delighted to know. I would hate it if you ran off with another woman."

That struck Otis as rather funny. It was better to run off with a BB gun, a motor scooter, a football helmet, and a toy fire engine than with a woman.

Then he thought about what T Caldwell had said about his father, and it wasn't funny anymore. What if Sally came down with a deadly liver disease because of what he had done?

"Bob Gidney told me that the specialist you saw at Ashland—isn't his name Russ Tonganoxie?—believes a lot of men your age, in your situation, want to run away to new lives, but few of them actually do it," Sally said.

"I helped a guy make fudge this morning, Sal. Can you believe that?"

"No, as a matter of fact. It's so unlike you, Otis. What kind of fudge?"

"Chocolate—even better than Grandmother Halstead's."

"Tell me about it."

"Not now."

"Where are you?"

"Not very far away."

"You really are alone?"

"For the first time in my life."

"Are you ever coming back from running away for the first time in your life?"

"I don't know."

They ended their conversation.

Otis felt like an even bigger fool. Here he was, the daredevil scooter man who had run away from home, and what did he do? Like a little fifty-nine-year-old, soon-to-be-sixty-year-old, boy missing his mommy, he called home after being gone only two days.

Within ten minutes, he was fast asleep.

That was because he'd remembered hitting his first baseball

when he was four, and because he'd finally come up with something to do about Church Key Charlie Blue.

OTIS WAS UP and gone before daylight.

He cruised by Johnny Gillette's, and as he approached Church Key Charlie Blue's, he slowed down. With only a few yards to go, he switched off the scooter's engine and coasted into the rim of the driveway.

With a stealth and precision that made him proud, he braked the scooter to a stop, disembarked, and lifted his Daisy Red Ryder air rifle from its hanging place.

Here we go, Buck.

He crouched down sniperlike behind the scooter, laying the gun across the seat as if it were the top of a trench or foxhole.

Tic-tac-toe, Church Key Charlie Blue!

Otis had remembered correctly that the front of Charlie's house had a window with nine small panes—a perfect tic-tac-toe board. Otis estimated the distance at about twenty-five yards, well within the range of this BB gun.

He sighted the window in the upper-left-hand corner and squeezed the trigger.

Pow!

The window cracked and the glass fell. Bull's-eye.

In rapid succession, he sighted and fired and hit the window in the lower-right-hand corner and the other two corners. Pow! Crash! Pow! Crash!

The center pane was splintered, and so were the four remaining ones on the sides.

Nine shots, all bull's-eyes.

Attaway to go, Buck!

As the last window crashed, Otis saw, out of the corner of his right sighting eye, the door to the factory side open. Here came Charlie.

In a flash, Otis hopped on the scooter, rehung the BB gun, kicked off the motor, and rode west again. Charlie was beyond running and, Otis knew, he also had no wheels.

"Oat-tus, you fucker!" he heard Charlie yell.

Oat-tus, without looking back, raised his right hand's middle finger high above his head as he rode out of sight.

There must have been times in Otis Halstead's fifty-nine years of life when he felt better than he did, but at that moment Buck couldn't think of any.

OTIS HAD BARELY noticed the police car when it passed him going the other way. The traffic was relatively heavy for old U.S. 56, but he guessed that was because, at almost eight A.M., people were on their way to work and to school.

He knew from his map that the road would be turning less traveled and more comfortable again before too long, before he came to the Chanute River Bridge detour that T had told him about. The only sights of consequence between here and the next real town, Cherryvale, the post-rock capital of the world, were that bridge, several crossroads with county roads, and mostly shells of tiny places between fields of growing wheat.

He was only a few minutes beyond Dearing when he first saw the police car in the small mirror attached to the left handlebar.

Then came the flashing blue lights on top of the police car as it came up behind him.

Otis pulled off the road, his mind racing with possibilities. Church Key? Could that thieving idiot have called the police about the BB-gunning of his windows? No way. He'd have to explain the four thou. What, then? The scooter was properly licensed, so it couldn't be that. Maybe he was driving the motor scooter over the posted speed limit? Or operating the scooter recklessly? Or had somebody riding a 1952 Pacemaker Cushman just robbed a bank or committed murder, and a serious case of mistaken identity was unfolding?

"Good morning, there, sir" were the first words spoken by the officer after he tossed away the cigarette he was smoking. He was dressed in a two-toned brown uniform, a matching straw Stetson, and brown shoes, with a pistol on his right hip and a gold badge on his left lapel that identified him as a deputy sheriff of Sabetha County, Kansas. On the right lapel was a small gold metal name tag that said CANTON. Otis figured his age at about sixty. He walked with a slight limp.

Otis returned the greeting and dismounted from his stopped scooter and put down the kickstand. "I hope I haven't done anything wrong, Sheriff," he said in as friendly and safe and unthreatening a voice and tone as he could manage.

"Not a thing but turn me green with envy," said Canton. "That's a Cushman Pacemaker, isn't it?"

Tonganoxie's male wheels thing again. Otis said, "It sure is— a 1952 model."

"I had an Eagle when I was a kid. It's what turned me on to motorcycles and then to law enforcement. I rode one for the Wichita PD for over twenty-five years before it spun out on me in an ice storm. Gave me a bum leg and a ticket out of town to a quieter life up here in the boonies. I rode escort when President Carter and Sandy Koufax and John Glenn and a lot of others came to Wichita and did several times when Dole ran for president."

The man was smiling, and so was Otis now. "Would you like to take my Cushman for a spin?" Otis asked.

"I thought you'd never offer. I would love it, I really would."

Otis stood aside, and the deputy climbed on the scooter with the grace, style, and strut of a motorcycle-escort cop. As they said in sports—he was back!

The happy Deputy Canton took the scooter out on the road and putt-putted west a few hundred yards, never out of Otis's sight, then turned around and came back.

"A fine instrument of transportation is what you have here," said Canton. While lighting a cigarette with a silver Zippo, he gave Otis a long hard look.

"What happened to your Chiefs helmet, friend?" he said. The attitude had changed subtly.

"I did a spinning-out of my own yesterday over at Marionville," Otis said, trying his best to keep things light, personal, nonchalant.

"Why don't you take that helmet off and let me have a good look at you?"

Otis took off the helmet.

Deputy Canton took his good look and then pointed back at the scooter. "What's the air rifle for?"

"Oh, just for playing around."

"You seem a little old for BB guns, football helmets, and motor scooters—that's what I'm thinking."

Otis smiled and took a step toward his scooter.

The deputy held up his right hand in a movement clearly marked: Stop! "Have you got a driver's license on you, friend?"

"You bet," Otis said, resisting to the urge to tell this man they were not friends. He retrieved his Kansas license from his billfold and handed it to the deputy.

" 'Otis Girard Halstead,' " the deputy read aloud. "You're a ways away from Eureka. Where you headed on that scooter of yours, Otis?"

Otis had trouble thinking of a time when he had been asked

a more difficult question. He knew that difficulties of an unknown but potentially serious type could lie ahead if he didn't give an answer that suited this Sabetha County deputy sheriff named Canton.

"Pagosa Springs, Colorado," he said.

"You got family there?"

"No, sir. I'm going to the Fred Harman Art Museum. He's the guy who created Red Ryder."

The deputy seemed to think about that a moment. He appeared amused, then confused, and finally said, "We've got a substation back down the road a couple of miles. I'd like for you to come with me, Otis. I'm not arresting you or anything like that. It's only a request."

"Why, sir?"

"So we can see about you."

See about me? "What is there to see?"

"Well, first, if there's a criminal possibility such as an outstanding warrant and then, maybe, if there's a mental thing of some kind."

Did people still escape from mental hospitals? Otis resisted an automatic desire to say something angry, resistant, smart—something that would only make matters worse.

"You up to following me on the scooter?" asked the deputy. "I'd suggest the other way around—you drive the cruiser and I drive the scooter—but they'd fire me for letting you drive the county's car."

In a few moments Otis, on his scooter, was traveling east close behind the deputy's car.

The initial possibilities that lay ahead were not hard to figure. Deputy Canton would do some kind of name check or something on Otis Girard Halstead and, with some calls, would determine that the scooter man with the Red Ryder rifle, Chiefs helmet, and Cushman was a runaway insurance company CEO/ civic leader. Then what? There was neither a criminal nor a mental possibility.

But. But who needs this? What self-respecting runaway scooter man would voluntarily put up with this kind of indignity?

Otis waited until there was a good clean break in the traffic and then swung the scooter around and headed west again.

In the handlebar mirror, Otis saw the brake lights of the deputy's car come on and the car pull off. Okay, so now what are you going to do, Mr. Deputy Canton? You have no legitimate reason to come after me, to take me into any kind of custody while you run your checks.

The sheriff's cruiser disappeared at a fast speed. Clearly, the deputy knew he needed more than the fact that here was a grown man acting like a child. That was not enough. He needed to run his checks, and he had decided to go to the substation as fast as he could to do it. He knew the Cushman moved very slowly, so if something did turn up, there would be no problem catching Otis.

Otis felt smart, quick, keen, clever, daring, cool—young.

NINE

OTIS BEGAN TO relax after a few minutes. There was no
Deputy Canton coming up behind him with flashing
lights, and the familiar had returned. The highway once again
had more bumps and cracks and rough patches on it than it did
cars or trucks or buses.

Buses. There were no buses. Otis had a vague notion that
Greyhound was about the only bus company left in Kansas, and
they sped by the small towns on the interstates from Kansas City
west across the state to Denver, and south to Wichita on into
Oklahoma. Buses were something that went with Red Ryder,
Cushmans, cast-iron fire engines, and wet dreams. In the '40s
and '50s, the crimson-and-cream buses of the Santa Fe Railway's
bus company, called Santa Fe Trailways, had been the major
form of transportation in and out of Sedgwicktown for Otis, his
family, and most everyone else he knew. The bus had stopped at
Hutchinson's Rexall in the center of town on Harper Street,
across from city hall, the bank, and most everything else that
mattered. Until college, Otis had left on every major excursion
of his life aboard one of those roaring machines that spewed
black smoke and blared with the sound of air horns and hissing

brakes. They were the magic chariots of escape, of tomorrow, of glory, of somewhere else. Now they were mostly no more.

And there came the first sign warning of the detour ahead for the Chanute River Bridge.

BRIDGE CLOSED AHEAD I MILE—FOLLOW DETOUR SIGNS.

The large black letters were emblazoned on a three-foot-square orange metal sign.

The signs grew in size and intensity as he got closer, the last being:

DANGER AHEAD. ALL VEHICLES MUST TURN LEFT.

There was a barricade made of orange barrels and heavy board slats across the road. Otis saw a red Dodge pickup and a blue Oldsmobile in front of him turn left as they'd been told.

But Otis decided not to do as he'd been told. Why not at least take a look at this old bridge? He was in no hurry. Deputy Canton had clearly turned up nothing that required a high-speed chase of a Cushman down old U.S. 56.

No car could make it around the barricade, but on the right—the north side—there was a gap large enough for him and his scooter to squeeze through. Otis dismounted and walked himself and pushed the scooter through the small opening.

Then he got back on the scooter and started riding. He could see the outline of bridge spans about a hundred yards ahead. There were the remnants of houses and stores on both sides of the road, but nothing that was still alive—structures or people. What small signs of life and business that may have remained had obviously departed with the closing of the bridge. The barricades made regular access impossible.

There were more barriers and warnings at the bridge, which Otis again walked his scooter around.

The last sign had the harshest words of all:

DANGER! BRIDGE UNSAFE!

PROCEED NO FARTHER!

TRESPASSERS WILL BE PROSECUTED!

STATE LAW!

At a glance, the bridge resembled something from truly ancient times. The half-circle steel girders that swooped up twenty-five or thirty feet on both sides were solid rust. So were the metal struts and stanchions and heavy wires that had been strung between and through the girders for reinforcement.

The bridge's narrow two-lane road appeared to be wooden planking, much of which was split, broken, torn, or rotted away.

The metal girders rose out of blocks of cracked concrete supports. On the right, faded and neglected, was a two-foot-square bronze tablet embedded in the concrete. Otis walked over and read it.

THIS BRIDGE WAS BUILT BY THE WORKS PROGRESS ADMINISTRATION UNDER THE ADMINISTRATION OF PRESIDENT FRANKLIN D. ROOSEVELT. IT WAS OPENED AND DEDICATED ON MARCH 12, 1936, BY U.S. SENATOR ANDREW MULVANE, U.S. REPRESENTATIVE HAMILTON HANOVER AND THE GOVERNOR OF KANSAS, RUSSELL MCDONALD.

Above it was a smaller green-and-white metal sign swinging loose by a single screw. It said: CHANUTE RIVER.

Otis stepped onto the bridge, being careful to put his feet down on what looked to be the most solid planks. He looked through the girders to the water of the Chanute River below. It was a long way down—fifty, maybe seventy-five feet—and the river was wider here—sixty yards at least—than Otis had expected. He must have driven over this bridge several times when he was younger, but he didn't recall it being this high or the river being this big or running this fast. Maybe it had rained upriver somewhere and the runoff had flooded the Chanute.

The current was really strong. He watched several cotton-wood limbs and what resembled a couple of large oil cans appear from upriver and quickly disappear below him and the bridge.

The only noise was that made by the flowing of the river.

He saw a few birds in the trees on the riverbank. They looked like meadowlarks, the state bird of Kansas, a fact that he had had to memorize in the sixth grade, along with the state tree, the cottonwood; the state motto, *Ad Astra Per Aspera*—"To the stars through difficulties"; the state colors, blue and gold; the state flower, the sunflower; and the state song, "Home on the Range."

Now, Otis. Sing, Otis, sing.

He began to sing in a southern nasal twang as loud as he could:

"Oh, give me a home,
Where the buffalo roam,
Where the deer and the antelope play . . ."

Then he stopped and switched to the other song of Kansas:

"I was born in Kansas,
I was bred in Kansas
And when I get married,
I'll be wed in Kansas.
There's a true-blue gal
Who promised she would wait,
She's a sunflower
from the sunflower state."

There. He had done it. He had sung again. He had sung, and his words were still reverberating and echoing out there some-where for the birds and any other living things around to enjoy, if they so desired.

He had never really ever sung a song—*any* song—by himself

since graduation day from high school. He had been the star male singer of Sedgwicktown High School, crooning à la Mercer at assemblies and gatherings, particularly "On the Atchison, Topeka and the Santa Fe," from the movie *The Harvey Girls.* That song was big everywhere but most particularly in small-town Kansas, through which the Santa Fe, as it was simply called, ran up, down, across, and through. Otis's ability to carry a tune with some skill was an accidental gift. Otis had joined the high school chorus because his mother made him, and he expected to mostly hum with the other boys behind the singing of the girls. But the chorus director, a woman named Alma Stockton, whose main job was to teach math, heard something special in Otis's voice. Alma Stockton told him many times that, for her money, Otis sang the Santa Fe song better even than Johnny Mercer, and he could probably make a living and life just singing that one song if he wanted to.

But Otis stopped performing after high school. He did not sing even a word of anything except later, as a Eureka civic leader, when he mumbled hymns at the First Methodist Church and "The Star-Spangled Banner" at Rotary, sporting events, and similar gatherings.

Now he had sung alone again as Johnny Mercer.

A crow, clearly attracted by the stunning beauty of the singing, landed on one of the girders that crossed over the bridge from one span to the other, high above Otis.

"Or are you a hawk or an eagle or a blackbird or a vulture instead of a crow?" Otis said to the black bird. He had never been good at distinguishing the really big ones. They all looked like crows to him.

He hoped it wasn't a vulture. He hoped there wasn't a carcass of a dead animal around that had drawn the attention of this bird, whatever its species.

He considered firing off a BB or two at the bird.

No, no. That bird wasn't hurting anything up there. Besides, it clearly appreciated the singing. So why bother it? But Otis was overcome with satisfaction in realizing for certain that he could have scored a bull's-eye on the bird's head if he chose to. He was that good with his Daisy rifle.

That was Buck, the marksman runaway singer—and an old cowhand? That reminded him of the Mercer song Pete Wetmore had said was his favorite.

Thinking maybe he was doing it in Pete's memory, Otis sang it loudly:

"I'm an old cowhand from the Rio Grande.
But my legs ain't bowed
And my cheeks ain't tanned,
I'm a cowboy who never saw a cow
Never roped a steer 'cause I don't know how
And I sure ain't fixin' to start in now
Yippie-yi-yo-ki-yay,
Yippie-yi-yo-ki-yay.
I'm an old cowhand from the Rio Grande
And I learned to ride
'Fore I learned to stand
I'm a ridin' fool who is up to date
I know every trail in the Lone Star State
'Cause I ride the range in a Ford V8
Yippie-yi-yo-ki-yay
Yippie-yi-yo-ki-yay."

Otis looked ahead to the end of the bridge, to the other side of the river. It wasn't really *that* far. The left side of the bridge's roadway seemed in better shape than the right. Fewer of the planks were missing or rotten. It was obvious that through the years, the winds and rain and snow from the north had hit the other side of the bridge first and done heavier damage.

If he was careful, he could drive his Cushman across. The alternative would be to go all the way back to the detour turnoff. What a silly and unecessary waste of time that would be. Onward, Otis.

Yippie-yi-yo-ki-yay, Buck.

He walked the scooter over to the left and confirmed that the planking looked much stronger and in better condition here.

Okay, Cushman, let's go.

He mounted the scooter, kicked the motor started, and began a slow, steady, careful putt-putt toward the other side of the river, keeping the scooter as close as possible to the metal span. Just in case.

Just in case he had to grab on to something.

No problems the first ten yards. He heard some cracking sounds but gunned the scooter quickly before anything happened. At twenty yards, not quite halfway, he spotted a missing plank ahead, right in his path. He swerved gently to the right and moved past it and then turned back onto his route.

Onward, Buck.

He felt terrific. He felt so good, so accomplished, so daring, so brave, so satisfied just knowing he could still sing a song like Johnny Mercer, blow the head off a big black bird with a BB if he chose to do so, or maneuver a motor scooter across an ancient, closed, dangerous bridge.

He saw the reflection of a flashing blue light coming from somewhere behind him. He turned to see what it was.

Crack!

The sound of splintering wood shot up from below the scooter's front tire. Otis jerked the handlebar hard to the right and threw the throttle all the way forward.

He felt the scooter giving way underneath him, the front first and then the whole machine. He desperately reached out to the side with his bare left hand for anything—a wire, a girder. Anything that he could hold on to, anything that would keep him from following the scooter down into the rushing waters of the Chanute River.

He had something in his hand. He wasn't falling. He held on as tight as he could. His body, from the waist down, was dangling through the roadway. A huge hunk must have come loose and given way. Maybe he could pull or swing himself up. He began to twist his body around so he could also grab something with his right hand.

"Hey, friend! Hold on! I'm coming!"

Who is that? thought Otis. *The voice is familiar. The deputy? What did he find on his computer check about me? Why is he here?*

Otis reached forward with his right hand. His left hand slipped free.

And down he fell. He screamed only once and only one word: "No!"

In the few split seconds it took him to hit the water, he tried to think of something from the fourth year of his life and saw off to the left what looked like his red scooter in the water, being rushed away by the current. Or was that a mirage? Wouldn't it have sunk like a rock?

Then he crashed into the water, feetfirst. The impact jarred loose the Chiefs helmet from his head. He continued down into the water like a rock.

Goodbye, helmet, Cushman, Red Ryder, wet dreams, Johnny Mercer, and life.

Water rushed into his mouth and nose, and he could no longer breathe.

TEN

H E HEARD A voice. A man's.

"Otis, it's me—Dr. Severy. Madison Severy. Call me Mad!"

A voice. A man's. Call me Mad? What does that mean?

I am not dead!

That's what it means.

I am not dead!

The words leaped to and through Otis. He tried to speak them out loud. Nothing happened. There was no sound. At least he didn't hear any. Were his lips moving? No way to tell.

He decided to open his eyes. But they wouldn't cooperate. It was like looking through a narrow, tiny mail slot in a foggy rain. Something like that.

He thought he saw filmy, poorly lit shadows. They were people, maybe—probably. Other people who, like him, were also alive. One of them was probably Mad.

I didn't drown!

He didn't try to say it this time. He just thought it.

"Otis, if you can hear me, nod your head!" The voice was male. It again sounded like the man who had said he was a doctor and should be called Mad. He was shouting. Why was he shouting?

I'm Buck, Mad.

Otis decided not to try nodding. He was too tired to do so even if he could.

"You're a lucky man," said Mad, his voice's volume turned down a bit but still very loud. "If that deputy hadn't happened along, there's no telling what the outcome might have been."

Call me Buck!

Otis remembered a man in a uniform. At the river. He suddenly had the taste of tobacco smoke in his mouth. Or was he imagining that? Did the guy do CPR?

He couldn't tell exactly where Mad was; the shouts had come from over there on the right. Mad must be screaming into Otis's right ear.

Stop that!

Otis figured his closed eyes might cause the Mad shouter to think this lucky patient of his had gone to sleep so he would shut up. He was wrong.

"He's reacting, he's coming to," said Mad in a much quieter voice. But not to Otis. Otis was the he. Mad was speaking to somebody else, probably one of those other shadows. Coming to?

I am not coming to!

"You've been saved, Otis," Mad said in only a half-shout. "Your driver's license got wet, but they could still read your name. Otis Halstead of Eureka, Kansas—you can thank God for that."

I don't thank God for anything!

"You're back home in Eureka at the Ashland Clinic."

No!

Otis tightened his closed eyes—or thought he did. That was what he wanted to do, at least. But he couldn't tell if he had done it. He couldn't tell if he had done—could do—anything.

"Look, look," said the voice of Mad, again to somebody besides Otis. "There's liquid seeping out from under his eyelids."

"Are those tears?" a woman asked. Was that Sally? Otis couldn't hear much better than he could see. Maybe that was why Mad was screaming into his ear. But it sounded like she really was crying. Sally always used to cry whenever Otis cried. She couldn't help herself. It was automatic. He cried, she cried. When was the last time that had happened—that he'd really cried?

"Tears of joy, obviously," said Mad.

"Maybe not," said another voice, also a man's. It sounded to Otis like it might be that idiot Tonganoxie.

Get me out of here, Idiot Tonganoxie!

Obviously, Idiot Tonganoxie couldn't hear that. Nobody could hear anything Otis was saying, because he couldn't talk. Right? Right, right.

Otis figured he might have had it all wrong. He wasn't alive at all. He had drowned in the Chanute. Now he was dead. But if he was dead, why would they have brought him to the world-famous Ashland Clinic? To study his water-soaked brain? Maybe Mad was lying to him. Or maybe Mad didn't even exist. Maybe the newly late Otis Halstead of Eureka, Kansas, aka Buck, was in some kind of anteroom on the way to hell. No question, the final destination for Otis was going to be hell. But maybe not Buck?

Different name meant different man meant different final destination?

There was only one way to find out what was really going on here.

He started with trying to move his right leg. Nothing happened. It wouldn't budge. Neither would the left. Or either of his arms.

I'm dead!

That smoking deputy was too late.

I'm only paralyzed?

Maybe he saved only my life. My brain's waterlogged—soaked through and through. Flooded to a standstill with water from the Chanute.

"I'm a neurotherapist, and I promise you we're going to bring you back to full life, if you do your part, Otis." It was Mad.

Could a neurotherapist, whatever that was, read minds—even those full of river water?

"Please try to move the big toe on your left foot. Otis, say to yourself: 'I am now going to move my big toe on my left foot.' "

My big toe on my left foot. Yes. I can say that to myself. I am now going to move my big toe on my left foot.

I'm alive!

"Move it, Otis. Move the toe."

Move it, Otis. Move the toe.

Otis tried but couldn't move it, at least as far as he could tell.

"Maybe tomorrow," said the male shadow called Mad to some other shadows, maybe those of Tonganoxie and Sally. "We'll give you something to help you sleep."

And they all went away.

OTIS TRIED TO jiggle his head around. He wanted to see if he could hear or feel water sloshing around up there inside his skull.

He neither heard nor felt anything, of course, and it was doubtful that his head had moved. But the thought might have made him laugh, or at least smile, if he could have done either.

Goddammit!

That was the prevailing mantra.

He was back in Eureka. And at the world-famous Ashland Clinic. Goddammit! Goddammit! Goddammit!

Maybe he'd have been better off without the deputy and the taste of the man's cigarette smoke in his mouth. Maybe he'd be better off drowned in the Chanute than alive in Eureka at the Ashland Clinic.

Yes, he was alive. He was pretty sure he knew that now. That was what he knew. That was all he knew. The last thought he'd had in the river was that he was drowning.

He didn't know about his Cushman, his Daisy Red Ryder air rifle, his cast-iron fire engine, and his Kansas City Chiefs helmet. Did they drown?

Why hadn't he drowned if they had? The deputy couldn't save them? Did he even try?

What about his singing again like Johnny Mercer? Did it drown, too?

He didn't want to be here as Otis. He was running away from here as Buck. He was going the other way. He was Buck who was going west on a motor scooter. Too bad they could read his driver's license. Maybe he'd be at some other hospital on the other side of the river if they hadn't figured out he was Otis Halstead of Eureka, Kansas.

Did they bring him back on the interstate? Buck didn't like interstates.

Goddammit!

Mad? Call me Mad? Is that nickname part of what passes for humor here at the world-famous Ashland Clinic?

Was Otis Halstead still fifty-nine? Or had Buck turned sixty?

Maybe the shadow people would tell him everything when they came back tomorrow.

Meanwhile, he would work on jiggling his right big toe. Or

was it the left one the shadow named Mad had wanted him to move?

Tears coming out of his eyes? That didn't make sense. He hadn't felt like crying. Only screaming. Maybe that was sweat Mad saw oozing from between the lids.

Or water left over from the Chanute.

THEN THERE WAS Mad again, talking.

"Good morning, Otis," he said. "I trust you slept well?"

Otis didn't attempt to respond, not with a nod or a wink, much less a word. He didn't know if he'd slept well or not or for how long.

What day was it? How much longer until his sixtieth birthday? Or had it already come and gone?

Mad was still talking.

"There's a young man out here who says he knows you as somebody named Buck. He says he saw your picture and read about your accident in the newspaper and decided to find you and come see you. He says his name is Tom but you know him as T. Injured people are often victimized by unscrupulous con men and women who read about somebody's misfortune. He seems terribly clean-cut, but one can never tell. He wants to come in and see you. Can you give us some indication of what we should do with him—what we should tell him?"

Some indication?

Otis wanted to move everything in his body, but not even his eyelids would budge. He couldn't get them to open any farther than the slit.

Let the boy in here!

Mad said to someone, "Well, I think in the interest of caution, we're going to have to turn the young man away. Sally said Otis had no friends like this kid—none his age anywhere. And his name certainly isn't Buck. This is Otis, of course."

Otis wanted to say to someone: Let him in. He *is* my friend. Buck's friend. Not Otis's. His mother is Iola, and she's dying. *Let the boy in here!*

He could not say that or give any signal—any indication—that would say it.

It made him wish that he were still in the river drowning—drowned, actually, by now. He hated the tobacco taste in his mouth.

"DO YOU FEEL this, Otis?"

Is it already another tomorrow? Otis recognized the voice and saw the shadow. It was a little clearer this time. The man—Mad again—was wearing a white coat and had a beard.

"I'm sticking a needle into the bottom of your right foot, Otis. Do you feel it?"

Otis felt it. Slightly. More like a small nick than a prick. Not enough pain to cause a grimace. Otis was in the slow process of deciding whether and how to acknowledge the feeling—assuming he could—when Mad said, "Obviously not."

Yes, obviously not. That, suddenly, was just fine with Otis. Obviously not.

Mad, plus whatever other human shadows were with him, disappeared again.

Fine, thought Otis. *Let them think I'm not feeling needle pricks or anything else. Let them think I'm not making progress. Let them think anything they want while I figure out what I'm going to do about being trapped in the world-famous Ashland Clinic.*

Trapped! I am trapped!

Now that they were gone, his mind wouldn't go to what he might do about his awful situation—alive but worse off than being drowned.

He moved on to trying to think of something that had happened during the sixth year of his life. Wasn't that where he was when he was falling into the river? Hadn't he thought of something from the fifth year? Or was he still on four?

Five was easy. That was the Christmas he didn't get the toy fire engine. So, six was he where he was now. He was six when he learned to swim underwater.

No. He broke his right arm when he was six. The break was just below the elbow. He wore a cast for several weeks. Everybody wrote their names on it. How did he break his arm? Did he fall from a tree or a truck or a tractor? He couldn't remember.

Seven. What happened when he was seven? Second grade. Oh, yes. Miss Sterling. Miss Sylvia Sterling. She was homeroom teacher and most every other kind of teacher. And he loved her. He really loved her. Most nights, the whole year he was seven, he imagined what it would be like to be with Miss Sylvia Sterling all his life.

His eighth year. He thought and thought. Nothing came. Nothing happened that he could remember. Not one thing!

Ninth? Wasn't he nine when he wrote the cornflakes ditties? No, no. That was the ninth *grade*. When he was thirteen or fourteen. Or something else.

What was the great one about Connecticut? Got it.

If I loved Hannah of Hartford,
And the phone went dead when we talked,
I'd ask the operator to re-Connecticut us.

OTIS WASN'T ABLE to count, but it was several—ten, twenty?—visits later that Mad said, "Otis, I'm going to assume that you can hear me and comprehend what I'm saying. We've run some tests, and that seems to be the case, even though you're not showing us the way we would have hoped."

Otis had to fight off a smile. He knew he could smile. That was one of many little movements he had made—only in private.

Mad, with an unfriendly edge in his voice for the first time, kept talking. Because Otis never talked, that left Mad to do it all. Mad seemed to do little else but talk.

"Let me tell you about what happened to you. We assume you know the first part. You fell through a break in the bridge into the water. A deputy sheriff happened by just after you fell. He went in the river after you and pulled you to shore. You were unconscious, and he did some CPR and brought you to. He was quite a hero, Otis."

Otis remembered the deputy sheriff. Not the name or the face but the brown uniform and the Cushman. He rode a Cushman. Was it his Cushman or Otis's Cushman? Was that him who yelled just before the scooter fell through the bridge? What had he found out about Otis on his computer? Quite a hero? CPR. Otis never learned how to do that. Some of the people at KCF&C learned. Some firemen came to the office and gave classes. Who wants to blow into a stranger's mouth? Not Otis. But that deputy blew his cigarette breath into Otis's. Quite a hero.

Mad kept talking.

"The deputy revived you, but only after your heart had

stopped—briefly. Only a short while, but long enough to cause problems, mostly of a neurological nature. We are confident that you will have a full and rapid recovery. Do you understand? Move your left big toe if you understand, Otis. Okay?"

Without thinking, Otis almost tried to move his left big toe. But he caught himself in time. He did not want to move his left big toe. Not yet. Assuming he could.

Mad said to someone else, "No movement. Maybe he's not understanding me after all."

Mad and somebody else—maybe more than one other person—talked among themselves, but they seemed to have moved away from Otis. He could hear only the sounds of their voices, not their words. Maybe they were whispering?

"Otis, I want to tell you about the deputy, the one who saved your life."

It was Mad again. He was back, talking right at and to Otis.

"His name was Canton. Phillip Canton. Everybody called him Phil."

Call me Buck!

"He was married and had three children and four grandchildren. He revived you and then, miraculously, summoned help on the portable two-way radio he had strapped to his belt. It was a miracle it didn't come off in the water and that it still worked after being in the water. All he got out to the sheriff's dispatcher was his location and something about there being an extreme emergency. Then he collapsed into unconsciousness himself, Otis. The exertion in the water triggered a massive coronary. By the time the emergency people arrived, he was dead. He died, Otis. There were attempts made in the ambulance, and again in the emergency room of the Cherrydale hospital, to revive him, but to no avail. He died saving your life, Otis. He was quite a hero."

Otis felt the breath of someone down in his face. *Is that you, Mad?*

"There are tears in his eyes! He's definitely crying this time! It worked! He understands!"

Yes, that was Mad shouting and breathing in his face.

Otis heard what sounded like cheers and applause from several people.

It didn't make sense to Otis that people would cheer and applaud about the death of a deputy sheriff named Canton who was quite a hero.

Then Mad said down into Otis, "Mrs. Halstead wants you to know that she had flowers sent to the deputy's funeral in your name—a large spray of roses—and that she wrote a personal note of condolence to his widow."

That made sense to Otis. Sally wrote all of the thank-you notes and saw to all of the sprays of flowers and gifts that needed to be sent. There were always sprays of flowers and gifts that needed to be sent.

That's what Sally did instead of acting in Inge plays.

Sally, where are you? Why aren't you down here in my face?

How will Sally know to send flowers and a note to T when Iola dies?

Now Otis remembered something that had happened when he was nine years old. He made all A's for the first time. And he caught a three-pound bass with only a tadpole as bait.

His tenth year was another nothing. He couldn't remember any specific thing from it. Not one thing.

But he did remember another cornflakes song.

If I loved Ann of Annapolis,
And she got sad and down,
I'd say: Cheer up, you're in Merry-land.

HIS DAUGHTER, ANNABEL, his only child, was there off to the right. Not Sally, his only wife. Otis felt Annabel's presence and heard her voice. He didn't have to see her to know that she was a pretty young woman—blond like Sally, with a good figure like Sally. Otis had always enjoyed her voice, which was slightly deeper than Sally's and those of most other females he knew. He'd always thought Annabel would have been a good actress.

Did I ever tell her that?

You have a great voice, Annabel.

"I'm here as part of your rehab therapy, Dad. The doctors think maybe I might be able to get you to talk. I told them that I didn't think so, but I'm here anyhow. I'm assuming you can hear me and understand me, so I am going to go on as if you do. Okay?"

Sure, fine. That's okay. Talk to me with your great voice as if I can hear.

"I don't have to tell you that we never talked much before, so why would we now? Neither of us really had a chance to need the other one to talk to, did we? I told the doctors that, but they believe everything's worth a try."

I've changed my mind. Don't talk to me. Please stop talking, Annabel. Please. I don't want to be here. That's why I ran away. Don't you get it? Doesn't anybody get it?

"So Dr. Tonganoxie—he's something strange, dressing like an old hippie grad student—said that some kind of jarring experience might be good for you. Speaking of jarring, I was really stunned that day you came home with the scooter. Mom had told me on the phone about the fire engine and the BB gun and the helmet. She said it was a second-childhood thing, and I told her it could be that it was your *first* childhood. When I saw you with the scooter, I knew I was right. You and the cop and Dr. Gidney were like three little boys riding and playing with that thing. I had never seen you so excited and so interested. I was right, wasn't I, Dad? All of that was part of a first childhood for you, wasn't it? I'm just guessing, because you and I never talked about anything like that, of course. Mom always said that because of the awful way your father died, it was best not to ask you anything about your growing up in Sedgwicktown. And I never did. Think about that. Here I am, you're my dad, and I don't know one thing about what your childhood was like. You never told me any stories about teachers or homework or sports or friends or family. That was as much my fault as it was yours. I could have asked you questions. I'm not complaining. You have a right to your privacy, your life. I never told you anything about me, either."

That's enough now, Annabel. Can't you see I'm asleep?

"I couldn't believe it when Mom called and said you ran away from home on that scooter. She seemed to be trying very hard to understand why you had done it. I understood. I'll bet you never had a chance—or you never took the chance—to do anything irresponsible in your whole life. So, suddenly, you decided to make up for lost time all at once. I understand. I'm sorry it didn't work out for you. I'm sorry you fell into the Chanute. But everyone—including Dr. Tonganoxie, who seems like the smartest of them all to me, by the way—swears you're going to be fine. I made them hold up their right hands and swear, and I believe them. So does Mom. Dr. Gidney has been really good with Mom, helping her get through all of this. He's spent a lot of time with her, talking her through it. She's fine. So am I."

Annabel fell silent. Otis couldn't tell what she was doing. But he knew she was still there because her shadow and her breathing and her sweet smell of perfume were still there. Wasn't it that French stuff she'd worn since high school?

"But maybe, as long as I'm talking, there are some things—really jarring things—that I did in the past that I didn't mention when they actually happened. You remember when I was sixteen and went away for the month of July to an Outward Bound trip through Montana and Idaho? I didn't really do that. I spent that month with a group of friends—boys and girls—robbing banks throughout Oklahoma and Texas. We hit twelve in thirty days. Just like the Bonnie and Clyde gang. I was the driver on most of the jobs, but toward the end, I went inside as a decoy and twice as an actual trigger girl. I shot two people with a machine gun, but they were only wounded. Flesh wounds, I think they called them, like in the movies. None of us killed anybody, which is good. And we got away with it completely. We needed the money to pay for the crack cocaine and other drug habits we had. I seldom went through a day without sniffing or smoking something. Did you notice anything strange about me around then? Must not have. The other thing I needed the money for was to have the twins. I had them one weekend at a hospital up in Kansas City—the Missouri side, of course—the next fall. The father was Reverend Garnett from church. It was hard keeping you and Mom from noticing I was pregnant, but I did it with sloppy clothes and then got lucky when the babies came early. I gave them up for adoption. But that does mean you've got a couple of twin grandchildren out there somewhere, probably in Kansas City. Both were boys, by the way. You could have played BB guns and everything with them. Sorry about all of that. Please don't get pissed at Reverend Garnett. It was all my fault. Just for the record, I also had two abortions and held up a 7-Eleven store to pay for them while I was an undergrad at KU. A Palestinian exchange student on the basketball team was the father the first time, a black football player—he did something in the backfield—from Wichita the second. Go, Jayhawks!"

Go, Annabel!

Otis had never in his life felt joy like this. He wanted to rise up from this bed and grab this funny, fabulous daughter of his, lift her up over his head like he did when she was a kid, let out a wail of love and pleasure, laugh until he cried, hug her until she squealed.

But he did nothing—said nothing, moved nothing.

He felt Annabel leaning over him, clearly in search of some reaction, *any* reaction. Her father kept his eyes closed, his face expressionless.

"You're asleep, aren't you, Dad? You didn't hear any of that, did you? Well, just in case you did, I hope you didn't believe any of it. Wow, that would have been some life if I had lived it. We responsible Halsteads don't do any of that, though, do we? Well, so much for trying the jarring experience—and, as the doctors said, 'aid in your father's rehab.' Good luck, Dad. Believe them when they say you're going to be fine. I'm so sorry you lost your scooter and toy fire engine and helmet in the river. You ought to find replacements when you're better. I'd be delighted to play with you. We never played much during my childhood, so maybe we can make up for it during yours—if you want to."

She leaned over him again. "You're really sound asleep, aren't you, Dad? I'd recognize that snore anywhere." She kissed him on his right cheek and left the room.

Otis stopped the faked snore and peeked out with a squint to confirm that Annabel was gone.

I ran away, Annabel. I can't come back—not yet. Not now. Maybe never.

ELEVEN? WASN'T HE eleven when Mr. Sam Troy, his principal, caught him taking a puff from a cigarette? Eleven or twelve.

It was eleven. There were five of them there in the parking lot back of school. Wes Lakin brought the matches and the cigarette, a Chesterfield he had stolen out of his father's pack. Wes lit it and then passed it around. Otis took two puffs in turn and, despite his best efforts to hold it back, coughed so hard he thought he would die. Mr. Troy called Otis's and the other boys' parents to school and told them what had happened. "Next time," said Mr. Troy, "these boys of yours will be expelled." Otis thought his dad might spank him, but he didn't. He only yelled at Otis while his mother cried. Otis promised never to smoke, and he didn't again until he was a sophomore at KU.

His twelfth year—sixth grade. There must be something to remember from that. Something good, maybe? Yes, he won the spelling bee.

Thirteen, thirteen—*thirteen?* Nothing.

Fourteen? Nothing except Julie Ann. He loved Julie Ann when he was fourteen. And she loved him.

When he was fifteen? He still loved her, but she left him for a guy with a Cushman. There were a lot of wet dreams. Fifteen was also the year he pleaded in vain for a Cushman of his own. And a football helmet. And a BB gun? No, that was back when he was thirteen. Or twelve, maybe.

Sixteen, all A's again. Nothing special there. Singing. He sang a lot in the choir and around town.

Seventeen? Skip seventeen.

Eighteen, nineteen, twenty, and twenty-one—college, in other words. Skip them all.

He remembered his wedding. The cake, a tall white edifice thing, got pushed off the table and jumped on and smashed into pieces and into a gooey mush by some kids. Sally's mother cried and yelled as if the cake were a person who had just died.

Annabel's birth. Certainly he remembered that. He was twenty-five years old. No, maybe twenty-seven . . . or twenty-six? Anyhow, he remembered when the doctor told him, "It's a girl, Mr. Halstead." No, that's not what he said. He said, "Congratulations, Mr. Halstead. You have a *Miss* Halstead." What exactly did the doctor say? Otis definitely remembered Sally screaming during labor.

The next few years? At work, mostly, talking, flying, thinking, worrying, hiring, firing, planning, deciding, flourishing. At home? On vacations? Nothing stuck out. He tried to go through each year again, beginning with right after the wedding.

Nothing much registered until he saw that toy fire engine at the antiques show. When was that? Just the other day, wasn't it?

Forget this. He was through trying to think of something that had happened in each year of his life. He wouldn't do that anymore.

"HI, OTIS. IT'S me, Josh Garnett, from church. Don't worry, I'm not here to administer last rites or anything like that. We Methodists don't do that kind of thing anyhow, do we, Otis?"

Leave me alone, please.

Otis had never had much of consequence to say to the Reverend Joshua Quinter Garnett, and falling into the Chanute River hadn't changed anything. Neither had Annabel's therapy-motivated jarring lie about Garnett. Otis saw him as an articulate, smart, good man who meant well, mostly did well, grinned too much, and was completely irrelevant to Otis's life.

"The doctors thought it might be helpful for me to talk to you, Otis. I realize that you and I were never what you would call great conversationalists with each other. That's interesting, because we're about the same age. I'm fifty-eight, you're fifty-nine . . ."

I am? Great! I'm not sixty yet!

Garnett paused in the apparent hope that Otis might speak or otherwise respond. Otis didn't, and the minister continued.

"I've always appreciated your support of the church with your financial resources and your willingness to serve more than once on our board. You've been chairman twice through the years, haven't you? I particularly appreciate that you are always there on Sunday morning at eleven—always in the third or fourth row, right in front of me. I must say, however, that once I began to think about it in preparation for coming here this afternoon, I was struck by a few things. I don't recall our ever having full eye contact while I preached a sermon."

I never heard one word you ever said—except "Amen" and, at the end of the service, "May the blessings of the Lord be with you."

"I also could not recall your ever really singing out loud. You always seem to know the words to most of the hymns without looking at the hymnal, but as best as I could tell, you only mouthed the words rather than sang them. Not everyone was meant to sing."

I was! I can sing like Johnny Mercer!

"Sally told me about the death of your father. She said you thought a God who could take away your father the way He did was not worth much. I would love the opportunity to talk about that when you are ready and able."

Never!

"I also fully understand why you carry some guilt over the suicide of Pete Wetmore. June Wetmore, I know, feels strongly that you were not always as thoughtful and supportive toward Pete as you might have been. I remember being quite stunned by your opposition to having Pete serve on the church board.

But don't be too hard on yourself, Otis. We're not into the confessional like the Catholics, but I would welcome talking to you about that as well."

Never!

Otis got stuck on the word "Catholic." There had been only a dozen or so Catholics in Sedgwicktown, but Otis knew them and liked them, and they'd been impressive enough to earn a place in one of his ditties.

> If I loved a Catholic in Boston,
> And she wanted a candle to light,
> I'd tell her to go to Mass-and-choose-it.

After Otis remembered that, he returned to listening to Josh Garnett long enough to hear the preacher's parting words.

"We Methodists, as you know, leave talk of being born again mostly to our Southern Baptist and other fundamentalist protestant brethren. But theology aside, there's something real and possible to the concept of starting life again—no matter one's age or situation. It's truly never too late, Otis. You can do it if you wish, right here in Eureka. I stand ready to help in any way I can. Goodbye for now, Otis."

Buck cannot be born again here!

OTIS PICKED UP a whiff of a soap that was startlingly familiar. He was delighted that he could recognize distinctive smells, as he had earlier with Annabel's perfume. It was another sign of progress that he would keep to himself. For now.

"Hello, there," said the voice that went with the smell. It was female, and it, too, was familiar.

Sharon? Could it be Sharon, the Beschloss-reading nymph by

Farnsworth Creek? He did not want to give away the fact that he could open his eyes and see pretty well. Not yet. So, through the lidded slits, he saw a woman in a white uniform. A nurse. There had been other nurses before. But they didn't smell like this one. Sharon had said she was a nurse. He'd never asked what kind of nurse she was.

Sharon, is that you?

"They tell me you won't even wiggle a toe for them," said the nurse. Was it Sharon's voice? Otis couldn't tell for sure.

Do you recognize me? I'm the old bald guy on the scooter! I was wearing that Chiefs helmet!

"One of the doctors thinks you're playing games with 'em, like a possum," the woman in white said. "I told 'em I bet I could get you to move a toe."

No!

Not even for Sharon, if it really was Sharon, would he do that. He had decided to keep his recovery mostly secret. He needed to work out a plan, to do some heavy thinking, about how to get out of here once his brain dried out a little more.

"Here it is," she said.

Otis felt something touching him. Was that Sharon's hand on his left big toe?

It is! Yes, it is! Sharon is fondling my toe!

Stop! Please, stop!

She said, "Oh my goodness, what is it that I see rising up there under the sheet?"

Otis knew what it was. He couldn't prevent *that* from happening.

Then she said excitedly, loudly, proudly, "You've had an erection, Mr. Halstead. I'm going to go spread the great news. Dr. Tonganoxie and Dr. Severy and everybody else will be so pleased."

All at once several people were in the room. Otis kept his eyes tightly shut, but he could hear them. It was a crowd.

"Congratulations, Otis," said Mad Severy.

"Yeah, congratulations, Otis," said Idiot Tonganoxie.

There was much applause.

ELEVEN

CONGRATULATIONS, OTIS.

That had been one of his father's favorite things to say. Whatever Otis did, good or bad, Dad had offered his congratulations. Sometimes he'd really meant it, as Mad Severy did now, sometimes he'd meant just the opposite, as in the spirit of Idiot Tonganoxie.

Now his dad probably would have been saying:

Congratulations, Otis, for driving your motor scooter into the river.

Congratulations, Otis, for not drowning and dying.

Congratulations, Otis, for causing that deputy sheriff to have a heart attack and die.

Congratulations, Otis, for having an erection after a girl half your age fondled your left big toe.

When Otis was growing up, the congratulations had been for forgetting to shut the door to the chicken coop, running over the cat, sweeping out the storm cellar, not making the football team, getting in to KU, crashing the tractor into the barn, being valedictorian of the class, being able to sing like Johnny Mercer.

The one thing Lucas Allen Halstead did not get to do was congratulate Otis for graduating from Sedgwicktown High

School. Lucas died on graduation day, before he had a chance to say, "Congratulations, Otis."

An unusually heavy thunderstorm, typical for late spring in Kansas, had brought much rain down on the Halstead place, just outside of town. No harm was done, though it left two inches of water on the cellar floor in the main house that Otis and his father decided to sweep and pump out before leaving for town. That, plus some unexpected mud holes at the end of their road, caused them to run late. In their haste, they went off without the Kodak Brownie his parents bought at Buck's in Wichita especially for taking photos at commencement, which because of the weather had been moved to the high school gym.

Lucas, the proud father of an only child, was determined to have photos of this event, so as the ceremonies were about to begin, he floorboarded the family Ford pickup back toward the farm. He figured he would have time to get there and back before Otis's valedictorian speech, which was to be something special in more ways than one. In addition to speaking a few words about the value and morals of hard work, Otis was going to lead the crowd in singing the "I'm a sunflower from the Sunflower State" refrain from "Sunflower" and then do "On the Atchison, Topeka and the Santa Fe" as a solo, his special Johnny Mercer way.

A twenty-two-car Santa Fe freight on the way from Hutchinson to the main line at Newton came through town just as the pastor of the Nazarene church gave the invocation. Otis heard the train off in the distance and thought it was a great coincidence that a Santa Fe train had come through at the best time to help him and his classmates graduate. Perfect sound effects.

A few minutes later, after the principal and the school board president spoke, Otis walked from his seat in the front row up and onto the stage. He was one of forty-seven graduates of the Class of 1955 before a crowd of about three hundred people.

He said his words, led the singing of "Sunflower," and sang his song about the coming of engine number forty-nine.

Otis looked for his father's face in the audience but was not alarmed when he didn't see it. Maybe Lucas was standing way in back and Otis had missed him.

After the commencement, Otis was asked by the principal and the Nazarene preacher to please come with them into the school building. His mother and some others were waiting to talk to him.

"There's been an accident, Otis," said the principal.

The "some others" were two county sheriff's deputies and a Kansas highway patrolman. Otis's mother, they said, was in an office next door.

The trooper did the talking. "Your father was trying to make the crossing there at the grain co-op before the train, and he didn't make it. I'm sorry, son."

One of the deputies, who looked vaguely familiar to Otis, said, "Lucas Halstead was a good man."

Lucas Halstead *is* a good man. No. He's no longer any kind of man.

Otis was not allowed to see the body of his father. Their blue Ford pickup had been compacted into a piece of flat metal with the forty-two-year-old body of Lucas Halstead smashed into a small, unrecognizable mess inside. That's what Otis assumed, anyhow.

Otis was overcome with what everyone told him were normal reactions. It seemed so unfair to kill a man on the morning of his son's graduation as valedictorian. Is there no God? If so, how could He do it with a Santa Fe train right before his son sang Johnny Mercer's "On the Atchison, Topeka and the Santa Fe" like Johnny Mercer?

Otis vowed right then never again to sing anything, much less anything by or like Johnny Mercer.

Everybody, most particularly the choral teacher, Alma Stockton, told him that didn't make sense. But to Otis, it was the only thing that day that made sense.

HIS FATHER'S DEATH also led to Otis's important first experience with the insurance industry.

"Florence, here is the check from Lucas's insurance," said the agent for Kansas Central Fire and Casualty. He was a local man named Pratt who was well known and well liked by the Halsteads and most other farm families around Sedgwicktown. He said, "The policy had technically lapsed, but the company agreed to pay up anyhow."

The policy had lapsed, but the company agreed to pay up anyhow?

Mr. Pratt explained to Otis's mother what had happened.

"Lucas had not paid the last six months' premiums because of what he said were some severe but temporary financial difficulties. We had no choice but to cancel the policy and notified him of the cancellation ten days ago. Our home office in Eureka, at my earnest suggestion following Lucas's tragic death, decided that it was good for the company to invalidate the cancellation and pay the death benefit. After all, Lucas had been paying on the policy for over fifteen years."

Otis knew there had been no money to buy a Daisy air rifle or a Cushman or much of anything else special, but he had not been aware of any severe financial difficulties. There had been several good rains during the growing season, and all 112 acres of the wheat crop had come in healthy and on time. The price at the co-op grain elevator where his father worked as the manager was geared to those in Kansas City and the Chicago commodities market, and they had stayed relatively high. So what was the problem?

Florence Halstead cried as she took the check for $12,500 from Mr. Pratt, and after he was gone, Otis asked her about the difficulties.

"Your father did something very irresponsible, I'm sorry to say," said Florence to her son. "He borrowed on everything we had, to invest in a scheme pushed by a man from Newton who came around the elevator. It failed, and we lost our money—every penny from the crop."

Otis asked what the scheme was.

Florence said she didn't know for sure.

Otis couldn't believe it. Here was her husband—his father—taking all of their money and investing it in a scheme, and she didn't even know what the scheme was.

Otis persisted, and finally, she said, "It had something to do with drilling for oil in northern Oklahoma—around Pawhuska, I think. Some Indian tribes were involved, too."

"Why would Dad do that?" he asked.

"He tried his best to keep it from you, Otis, but your father really hated being a farmer, and he hated managing the elevator even more," said Florence. "He had been on and around farming all his life, but he really wanted to do something else."

"*What,* exactly?"

"He had no idea. But he figured with some more money, he would be able to come up with an idea. Once he mentioned moving to a city—Wichita, in particular—and working at Boeing, Cessna, Beech, or one of the other airplane factories."

Otis the seventeen-year-old could not imagine what life in a city would be like. He was even nervous about living in Lawrence, where KU was, and Lawrence was a fourth the size of Wichita.

But now, in a bed at Ashland Clinic, Otis was remembering the conversation for what it said about his father, not about possible life in the city. He knew about inherited traits and tendencies because they were a part of assessing risk in the insurance industry.

Insanity can be genetic, he knew. But can a son inherit from his father a desire to run away? Can panic be passed on? How about a chromosome for turning back into a child at an advanced age?

Is there such a thing as a Cushman motor-scooter gene?

Otis figured he might ask Mad Severy or Idiot Tonganoxie or somebody else at the clinic when he was able—and willing—to ask anybody anything ever again.

He also had a rare thought about his mother. Why did he never wonder about getting any genes or something else important from her? Why was she so small, so insignificant, in his memories and worries and dreams, even now? All he could remember was her either going along with Dad or explaining Dad. She never seemed to think or do anything on her own.

He could ask these Ashland shrinks about his mom. Maybe there was some syndrome that would explain why she'd left such a faint impression on him and his life. Was it a syndrome about her—or him?

And what about singing? He remembered singing something just before he fell into the Chanute. Yes! He thought it was "Home on the Range." Or was it "Sunflower"? Yeah. For Sharon. Could he ever do that again?

These were terrible things to think. But thoughts about never singing or talking or walking or doing much of any living again were beginning to go away for Otis. There had been enough progress—even before the glorious erection—for him to believe he was going to be all right.

I'm going to be Buck again!

So maybe that deputy sheriff named Canton hadn't made a terrible mistake, blowing in Otis's mouth. *Thanks for not letting me die, Deputy Canton. Otis thanks you. Buck thanks you. But there's a problem. Buck's back here in Eureka as Otis. Unless he can think of some way out of here, you may have died a hero for nothing, Deputy Canton.*

Maybe the way out was suicide. In his present condition, Otis might be able to pull the trigger of a pistol like Pete Wetmore had, if he had one. He might also be able to move his hands and arms enough to take an overdose of pills, assuming he could get any pills strong enough to kill him. But he couldn't cut his wrists or tie a noose from sheets and hang himself from the ceiling. Not yet. He couldn't jump from a window or throw himself in front of an Atchison, Topeka, and the Santa Fe train.

Bad thought about the train. Dad didn't throw himself in front of that Santa Fe freight. It was an accident. Just like falling through the Chanute River Bridge was an accident.

Otis's dad had an accident on the Atchison, Topeka, and the Santa Fe.

It wasn't your fault, Johnny Mercer!

Maybe Otis could get somebody else to do the killing for him. Maybe Sharon would stab him in the heart or wrap a cellophane bag around his head. Or beat him to death with a Beschloss book.

But until he started talking, he couldn't ask her. Not only about killing him but also about committing another, most important act.

He so longed for her to touch him in other places—other, more intimate, sensitive places. Only the left toe. She only fooled with his left toe. *Who was that idiot Clinton adviser who paid a Washington prostitute to suck on his toes?*

Otis figured he might pay a prostitute to blow into his mouth but never to suck on his toes.

Why did he use the word "idiot" so much? Everybody was an idiot. Where had he picked up that word? Pete Wetmore might still be alive if Otis hadn't called him an idiot and treated him like shit.

Otis vowed to work on not calling people idiots anymore. He'd spread it around. Moron, fool, jerk, dope. How about shit-head? Not a good Kansas word, by any means. But he'd heard it in Kansas from a GI Bill student at KU who had been a marine. He called everybody, even his best friends, shitheads. Yeah. From this day forward, Otis would call everybody a shithead. He wouldn't call anybody anything right now—not out loud, at least. But he would *think*-use the word about people he didn't particularly like. People such as Tonganoxie. How did that shit-head ever make it through medical school or shrink school or wherever he went? Mad Severy seemed okay. He was neither a shithead nor an idiot.

Neither was the lovely Sharon. There was a problem with her, though. Otis was not absolutely sure the young nurse in the white dress was Sharon from the Farnsworth Creek. He hadn't gotten a really good look at her. And there on the creek bank, she was in jeans, not a white nurse's uniform.

Otis had worn a uniform once.

HIS WAS A dark blue uniform of the U.S. Navy.

In 1955 there was a draft-induced imperative for every male college student to do some military service. Otis chose the Naval ROTC at the University of Kansas, but he broke an ankle in a pickup basketball game at the beginning of his senior year. That resulted in his being declared physically unfit for service. He didn't mind because he hadn't really been that keen on being a navy or marine officer, or any other kind of military person.

But if it hadn't been for that ankle injury, he would not have been in the student infirmary the evening Sally came in to play the part of Cherie from *Bus Stop.*

Instead of going into the service, he went directly from KU, with his bachelor's in business administration, to work. He had five solid job offers, all but one from Kansas companies or firms—two banks, a finance company, and an insurance company—that wanted him to work for them in Kansas. The outsider proposal came from United America Seating in West Orange, New Jersey, one of the world's largest manufacturers of car, truck, and bus seats. Their corporate recruiter came to Lawrence in search of young men who, he said, "saw opportunity in sitting down."

Otis saw no such opportunity, and he had absolutely no interest in moving to New Jersey. He went for an interview with the seating man because the dean of students insisted that every senior go through at least one interview with a foreign or distant company for the experience. Otis chose the New Jersey seating company over a mortgage company based in Minneapolis and an outfit that had been hired to establish a banking system in Nigeria.

"Let me first tell you that from your office window, you will be able to see the Manhattan skyline," said the seating recruiter, whose name was Charles Michel. "Don't think New Jersey— think Broadway, the Great White Way, Central Park, the Empire State Building, the Waldorf-Astoria, 'New York, New York, it's a wonderful town.' "

Otis tried, but all he could think of were muggings, bums, honking horns, dirty rivers, polluted air, crapping dogs, the Yankees, and rude people. He hadn't been to New York or New

Jersey, and his thoughts, impressions, and imaginings were based solely on what he had read and heard.

"Seating is a forever industry—it's of the past, present, and future," said Michel, a well-dressed man of forty or so with a slight waistline problem that made Otis think he had spent too much time sitting down on United America seating. "No matter what happens, in times of war or peace, depression or prosperity, people have always had and always will have the need for something to sit on as they move from place to place. It's like schools and teachers."

Otis said he didn't follow the analogy. Michel explained, "There will always be sexual intercourse between men and women, which means there will always be children, which means there will always be schools, which will always require teachers."

Otis found himself listening to the man. He actually began to think about moving to a place called New Jersey and selling seating and looking out at the tall buildings of New York City. He began to seriously wonder if that might be the most exciting thing for a newly educated farm boy from Kansas. His widowed mother had taken her insurance money and moved to Wichita, where she had made a new and comfortable life as a salesclerk in the women's clothing department at Buck's, then the largest and best department store in Kansas. Otis had gotten himself through college with scholarships and part-time jobs at Lawrence cafeterias and doughnut shops, so she had no lingering obligations to him. She had a sister and many friends in Wichita, so she didn't need her son close by.

Why not take a risk and go to New Jersey and the Great White Way? But his father might have said, Congratulations, Otis, on running off and leaving your mother in Kansas.

Congratulations, Otis, for taking a really big risk.

Another angle on risk was at play. Kansas Central Fire and

Casualty of Eureka had offered him a life's work dealing with the calculations of risk that underlay the insurance industry. Otis also liked the KCF&C recruiter who came to campus. He was younger than the seating man by about ten years and was a native of Pennsylvania.

"I had to leave home to find the Land of Oz and opportunity," he said to Otis. "You're already here. Come with me to be a man of KCF and C."

He said it in the same tone the fundamentalist preachers in Sedgwicktown used at the end of the Sunday-morning service when they invited people to come down and give their lives to Jesus and join the church.

Otis had never forgotten what Pratt of KCF&C had done for his mother, and that played a major role in his decision to accept the invitation. The company that had paid off Lucas Allen Halstead's death benefit when it didn't have to was a company of compassion and quality.

There was something else at work, Otis realized now in his hospital bed as he flipped through it all. What was it T Caldwell's mother had told him? There are those who are meant to leave and those who are meant to stay. Otis was meant to stay.

Last September he had celebrated having stayed in Kansas with the same company for thirty-eight years. He had stayed, all right.

Then came the cast-iron fire engine and all the rest, and here he was, a prisoner of sorts at the Ashland Clinic.

But what about Sally? What had happened to her desire to be an actress? He couldn't remember their having a really serious conversation about it. Nothing more than a few minutes here and there. They fell in love, he proposed, and they talked from then on about his job offers and waiting awhile to marry but not about her acting.

Why didn't they talk more about her acting?

What if they had gone to New Jersey thirty-eight years ago? Would he still be working at United America Seating? Would he be the CEO? What kind of life would Sally have had? Would she have crossed over the river to Manhattan to be an actress? What about Annabel? She was working on getting a master's in social work at KU. What would she have been doing or studying—and where—if she had been born and raised in New Jersey instead of Kansas? Would she speak with a New Jersey accent instead of in that flat Kansas way? Would they have talked to each other? Would he and she have been a real father and daughter?

Would he have wanted to run away from New Jersey? To the West? Wouldn't it have been hell getting away from the New York–New Jersey area on a 1952 Cushman Pacemaker? He could imagine the traffic, the trucks, the smog, the turnpikes, the road rage, the idiots—the shitheads. Would he have bought a New York Giants or Mets helmet instead of a Chiefs helmet? What about the Daisy air rifle? They were anti-gun nuts up there in the East, so he probably couldn't even have bought one without being arrested. Buck definitely would not have worked as a new name. There probably wasn't one Buck in the states of New York and New Jersey put together.

What kind of person would I be now if I had gone away to New Jersey instead of staying in Kansas?

Would Pete Wetmore still be alive? Would Pete have killed himself, somewhere else working for somebody else?

What about Deputy Canton? Would Canton have had a heart attack anyhow? He was a smoker and overweight and, according to all health and insurance industry paradigms, his chances of dying from a myocardial infarction were in the highest percentile.

Otis saw something up on the hospital room ceiling that was shining, sparkling. It appeared to be a decoration of some kind. A red and green and silver star? Was it a Christmas thing?

It couldn't be. This was still May. Only a few days before his birthday.

Christmas.

Last year, at the small annual Christmas luncheon Otis gave for the KCF&C's top eight executives in a private dining room at the Hotel Eureka—there was also a huge company party for everybody—somebody suggested they go around the table and each recount his or her most memorable Christmas.

The stories were mostly happy ones. The time somebody's father came back from World War II and they had Christmas for him two months late—the best Christmas in the family's history. The Christmas it snowed twenty-two inches and everyone was snowed in for almost a week of eating, singing, and rejoicing. The time somebody forgot to turn on the oven to cook the turkey and everybody had hamburgers from a Kings-X diner instead. And so on. Otis's story was about not getting the Daisy air rifle he wanted so badly for Christmas. But he told it with a light touch, so it didn't violate the joy-to-the-world spirit of the lunch.

Only Pete Wetmore, the last of the eight to speak, told a real downer.

"On Christmas Eve when I was seven, my parents went down the street for a quick open house some neighbors were having. While they were gone, my little brother and I decided to scour the house for Santa Claus presents. We already knew there wasn't a Santa Claus, but we had not let on to our folks. We were playing along with them. We found our presents in a closet in the basement, right where we thought they might be. There were a lot of great things in the closet, including the Sandy Koufax baseball glove I wanted with all my heart, and the twenty-seven-soldier war set my brother had written to Santa for. When Mom and Dad came back, they sensed something from our looks or attitudes or giggles. They asked if we had been looking around the house for anything. We both lied. Dad, who'd had a little eggnog at the open house, went down to the basement and saw signs of our having been in the closet. He came back upstairs, knocked both of us down with his fists, and then went over to the Christmas tree, pulled it down, and said as far as he was concerned, there would be no Christmas in the house this year. He went into our guest bedroom and stayed there the rest of Christmas Eve and all day Christmas. My poor mother cried and cried, pleaded and pleaded with him to come to his senses. My brother and I shouted our apologies and vows of perfect future behavior through the bedroom door, but to no avail. My mother, brother, and I had a form of Christmas late in the morning, opening the few presents that were under the tree. We stood the tree back up, but most of the decorations had been broken or bent. We never were given the things that were in the closet, including my Koufax glove. That was my most memorable Christmas."

There was absolute silence in the room when Pete finished.

It was Otis who finally broke that silence by saying, "Think of it as a learning experience, Pete."

Think of it as a learning experience, Pete?

Recalling his words now as he looked up at what appeared to be some kind of Christmas decoration, Otis would have given anything, including possibly his own life, not to have said such an insensitive-shit thing to Pete Wetmore.

But that was only one of many, many shit things he had said and done to Pete. Intentionally keeping him out of meetings or business dinners he knew Pete wanted to attend. Not inviting

Pete and his family to various high-visibility social events, and never having them to the Halstead home. Cutting off Pete during meetings with cracks like "Boring us to a decision, Pete?" Keeping Pete out of membership in the most exclusive men's club in Eureka. Even blackballing him from being on the board of their church.

Was it the bald thing? What if Otis had not lost his hair? What if he had not ruined his ankle and been a navy or marine officer? Would he have been different?

Would he still have treated Pete like shit?

Would he still need to be Buck?

TWELVE

EVERYONE SEEMED TO know about Otis and Pete Wetmore.

Mad Severy, the rehabilitation provocauteur, used it as a shock therapy tool. He said to Otis, "I've been told you pretty much caused a man named Pete Wetmore to kill himself. Some might say that was a form of murder. Isn't that right, Otis?"

Otis shook his head to the left and then to the right.

It was a reflex response. A real one. If Otis had realized he could move his head, he might have decided to nod up and down, saying yes.

Whatever, it was considered another erectionlike break-through event in the coming back to life of Otis Halstead.

Otis, again, was alarmed a bit at the happiness over his response to something concerning the death of another man. On the other hand, he understood what was going on. Response was everything. Whatever shocks it took to get him to respond were part of the cure, part of bringing him back to life.

"Now you wish you'd said yes, don't you, Otis?" asked Mad, who was clearly one astute man. "Say it. Say yes and nod."

Otis nodded. He figured, why not? Give them another thrill.

"You can move your head," said Mad Severy. "Add that to the list with erecting—if that's the word—when properly stimulated by Jeannie, and we've got progress on our hands, Otis."

"Sharon," Otis blurted out. This time the shock had worked. "Sharon" was spoken in a full-throated voice like that of a normal human being.

He had talked out loud for the first time since falling into the Chanute.

"Hey, Otis! You did it!" said Mad Severy, a most happy man. "Go on. Tell me more. Sharon who? Sharon what, Otis?"

Sharon the nurse, you idiot. Sorry, you moron.

But those words were not spoken.

There had been enough dramatic progress, public and private, for one day—for a few moments of one day.

And when they were over, what lingered with Otis were thoughts about Pete Wetmore, not Sharon.

OTIS HAD MET Pete the first time over dinner at the Oak Room, a famous and expensive restaurant at the Presidential Shore Hotel in Chicago. A headhunter firm had spit out five finalists for a new KCF&C executive vice president, one who had CEO potential and probabilities. Otis decided to go to each of the five by himself before involving board members and others in the company.

Otis was never quite at ease in elegant restaurants like the Oak Room. He always felt slightly like a Kansas farm boy, slightly out of place, slightly afraid he might do or ask for the wrong thing. But he loved the feeling of well-being, of success, of arrival that being in such places gave him.

In contrast, the initial thing Otis noticed about Pete Wetmore was how at home he appeared. Pete took a menu from the waiter as if it were a natural act, something he did as regularly and as casually as opening a door or shaking a right hand.

Pete ordered asparagus tips with a light Belgian hollandaise sauce to start and, for the entree, beef Wellington—medium well—in a calvados sauce with skinless new potatoes seared in avocado butter.

"I'll have the same," Otis said as nonchalantly as he could manage. It annoyed him that he felt awkward in this situation. After all, he was a college graduate, and he had been in business for over thirty-five years, he had traveled, and *he* was the corporate CEO at this dinner table. But the feeling of country hick would not go away—not at this particular moment in the company of this particular young man.

The wine steward was at the table a few minutes later to make it worse. He was a man in his forties who could have passed for a corporate CEO in both appearance and speech. Otis said he was no wine expert and insisted that Pete choose a wine that fit their meal choices.

Yes, a red would be perfect, they agreed. Something light and five years old from Bordeaux.

As the staff of the Oak Room went off to prepare the wine and the asparagus, Otis immediately turned to the business at hand, to his turf, to his world, where he felt very much at ease and where he was in charge.

"Why are you interested in coming into the insurance business?" he asked Pete firmly.

"I need a new challenge," said Pete. "Mortgage banking has its high moments, but I believe I have now experienced and learned most of what there was to learn from them."

Otis already knew about Pete's background from the search people. Pete was the product of an upper-middle-class life, having grown up in a nice Denver suburb, the son of a Chrysler dealer and a garden-and-country-club-golfing activist. Mother and father had attended the University of Colorado at Boulder, where they had met, but they had higher and lawyer aspirations for their two sons, both of whom went to Ivy League schools. Pete's was Harvard, where he graduated in the upper third of his class and went on immediately to Harvard Law School, where he did almost as well. He had practiced law for a couple of years and then gone into mortgage banking.

Otis asked about hobbies and outside interests.

"None, really," said Pete.

"Do you follow sports?"

"Not much, except the Cubs sometimes."

"In Eureka, you'd have to cheer for the Royals in baseball and the Chiefs in football, or you'd get run out of town."

Pete smiled but said nothing. Otis couldn't get a reading on what the smile meant.

"Family," said Otis. "Tell me about your immediate family— wife and kids."

Pete said his wife, June, whom he had met at Harvard, as his parents had done at Colorado, was not happy in Chicago. They had the kids and she had gotten caught up in the mommy-wife-homemaker trap. Her bright mind, talents, and energies were being consumed by preschool, school, after-school, playgroups, soccer, baseball, carpool, sleepovers, Cub Scouts, Sunday school, Junior League, grocery shopping, meals, homework, cleaning ladies, yardmen, babysitters, fistfights, pouts, sore throats, skinned knees, hundred-degree temperatures.

Otis considered telling Pete that Eureka, Kansas, had all of those things for bright wives and mothers, but he decided against it. That was about something very personal between this young man and his wife, and it had nothing to do with geography or place. Otis knew all about that kind of thing from his own life with Sally, who had lived a similar life. But she didn't consider it a trap.

Or at least Otis didn't think she did. They had never really talked about it. They had never really talked about much of anything important. Their life had become one of mutual assumptions rather than of discussions. And it worked. Or at least it worked for Otis. And he assumed it did for Sally.

Pete passed on dessert. So did Otis. Both had a double decaf espresso.

"A brandy or another after-dinner drink?" asked the waiter.

"No," said Otis first. Pete ordered a VSOP cognac just for "the sniff." When it came, all he did was run it back and forth under his nose several times. Otis had never seen anybody doing such a thing—ordering a sixteen-dollar glass of cognac and not even taking a sip of it.

Over the next few weeks, Otis had similar dinners in Omaha, Boston, Hartford, and San Antonio with the other four executive vice president finalists, all of whom were already in the insurance industry. Then the more formal selection process began. Eventually, Pete and the others were viewed, interviewed, and assessed by a special committee of the board of directors and then individually by all twelve members of the board. A fairly solid consensus emerged for Clyde Oakley, a forty-three-year-old vice president of United Services Automobile Association, or USAA, as it was called, the high-quality multiline San Antonio company that began years ago as an auto insurance company for active-duty military officers. Oakley was a quick, trim, impressive Annapolis graduate who had served as a nuclear submarine officer for five years before leaving the navy and joining USAA.

Only Otis dissented on Oakley. He insisted on Pete Wetmore.

Why? Why, why, why? everyone asked. Wetmore was ranked fifth out of five by everyone else involved in the search. Why

Wetmore? He had no insurance experience, no outgoing com-
mand personality, no nothing except a couple of Harvard
degrees.

Why Wetmore?

Thinking about it now as the man who had almost drowned
in the Chanute River, Otis began to wonder if maybe he'd
wanted Pete Wetmore as his number two so he could treat
him like shit.

But before he could go any further toward a final answer, he
had to deal with a woman who was here in his hospital room
screaming at him.

"YOU LYING SHITHEAD!"

Sally's face, breath, and smell were right down on him.

*Where have you been, Sally? Annabel came. So did Josh Garnett,
offering to help me be born again.*

"Who the hell is Sharon?"

Sally's yell was loud and shrill.

He could see her features, but even if he couldn't have, he
would have known for sure it was Sally. He knew her aura and,
most particularly, her breath as well as he did everything else
about this woman he had made a life with. Her breath had a
unique natural sweetness that beat anything Colgate or Crest
could create. Not even raw onions on a cheeseburger or a plate
of spaghetti covered with a garlic-saturated tomato sauce could
cause him to turn away from her open mouth.

Why had she waited so long after the accident to say anything
to him?

But her words didn't make sense. Shithead? That was *his* new
word. She hadn't ever cussed like that. Had she caught the same
thing Pete Wetmore did before he killed himself? Had she, too,

come down with a case of the syndrome named after some Frenchman?

Otis wanted to say: Sharon's a young woman—a kid, a child—I came across on the bank of Farnsworth Creek who wouldn't run away with me. She wouldn't be my sunflower from the Sunflower State. She said she was a nurse, and I thought she was the nurse taking care of me here. That's all there is to it. She touched my left big toe, and it caused me to have an erection. A real Sunflower erection, you might say. That's all. Well, maybe not quite all. Thinking about her also brought on a wet dream in a motel the other night somewhere this side of the Chanute River Bridge. But that's it. I promise. She's a sunflower from the Sunflower State to me, but I'm only an ugly bald-headed old sunflower man to her. An ugly bald-headed *dirty* old sunflower man, to be even more specific—probably.

These words—all of them—were forming in his mouth. They felt close to coming out as complete sentences and thoughts. Maybe his full power of speech was on the verge of returning?

But he decided not to test it. Not yet—not now.

Sally spoke again. "You told me there wasn't a woman involved in your silliness, your running away like an idiot on that silly goddamn scooter with that silly goddamn football helmet and silly goddamn BB gun. You lied, you goddamn shithead, Otis."

What's happened to your sweet mouth, Sally?

Otis thought that maybe he wasn't hearing correctly. Maybe she was saying these things in her normal, civilized, unprofane way, and he was hearing her wrong. Could there be another syndrome discovered and named by another Frenchman that affected the people on the receiving end? Could there be a disease that caused people to hear cusswords that weren't really spoken? Somebody uttered a completely innocent word such as "sweetheart," and the listener heard "shithead"?

The other possibility was that he didn't know Sally as well as he thought he did. Maybe she talked this way to everyone but him. What was it Pete Wetmore had said about his use of "fucking"? That he had never talked that way to Otis. Or maybe Sally had always been prepared to talk this way but had never been angry enough to do so until now, until this, until Sharon.

Otis felt something. A touch, a hand. The hand was down on his most sensitive private parts.

"Is this what Sharon did for you, Otis?"

Otis shook his head.

"No need to shout, Otis," Sally said.

Call me Buck!

Sally put her mouth to his. "Kiss me, you lying shithead," she said softly, quietly, soothingly, invitingly. "Shithead" had never been uttered so lovingly, so fetchingly.

He kissed her back as hard as he could.

"You're going to be fine, Otis," she said.

You're going to be fine, Otis?

Well, yes and no. Fine, yes, in that he may be headed toward living again. Fine, no, in that he may also be headed toward living again the old way in Eureka, Kansas, as Otis Halstead. He couldn't do that.

Buck couldn't do that!

Otis considered whether he might find and buy another toy fire engine, order another Daisy air rifle, and replace his drowned scooter with a Pacemaker or with some other Cushman model. He decided he definitely would not get another Kansas City Chiefs helmet. No, this time he would get a New York Giants or Jets helmet.

Sing, Otis, sing!

That's it! I'll sing instead of talking. Eureka!

He opened his mouth and sang with his Johnny Mercer twang and tone:

"We meet and the angels sing
The angels sing the sweetest song I've ever heard.
You speak and the angels sing
Or am I reading music into every word?"

Sally raised her head off his chest and exclaimed, "My God, Otis!"

Otis smiled.

"You're talking—singing!"

Otis just kept smiling.

"I didn't know you could sing!"

Otis hummed.

Sally said, "You sound just like somebody famous! Is it Tennessee Ernie Ford?"

Otis shook his head vehemently.

"Steve Lawrence?"

Otis shook his head even more.

"I know, I know. Hoagy Carmichael."

Otis moved his head but not so vehemently. She was getting close. Hoagy Carmichael, the man from Indiana, and Johnny Mercer, the man from Savannah, had been friends and collaborators.

"Got it, Otis. Johnny Mercer. It's Johnny Mercer—the happy guy."

Otis nodded vehemently.

"You're a wonderful Johnny Mercer," Sally said. "It's a miracle."

Otis smiled.

"I don't know what to say," said Sally, still clearly surprised, shocked, unbelieving. "Why have you never sung like Johnny Mercer before?"

Otis did nothing.

"Why have I not acted anymore? You could ask me that, too, if you wanted to," Sally said.

Then Otis sang:

"Do you hear that whistle down the line
I figure that it's engine number forty-nine
She's the only one that'll sound that way
On the Atchison, Topeka and the Santa Fe.
See the old smoke risin' 'round the bend
I reckon that she knows she's gonna meet a friend,
Folks around these parts get the time of day
From the Atchison, Topeka and the Santa Fe.
Here she comes . . . woo-oo-woo-oo-woo-oo-woo-woo,
Hey, Jim, you better get the rig,
Woo-oo-woo-oo-woo-woo,
She's got a list of passengers that's pretty big,
And they'll all want lifts to Brown's Hotel
'Cause lots of them been travelin' for quite a spell,
All the way from Phil-a-del-phi-ay
On the Atchison, Topeka and the Santa Fe."

Sally thrust her head down on his chest and sobbed. "Oh, Otis, I love you, I love you. You're back, you're back. You came back, Little Otis."

Little Otis?

Who?

Back?

Never!

With her face away from his chest, Sally said, "Do you recognize this, Otis?" She shook her shoulders, cleared her throat, and said dramatically, " 'You picked up the javelin real careful like it was awful heavy. But you threw it, clear, *clear,* up into the sky. And it never came down again. Then it started to rain. And I couldn't find Little Sheba. I almost went crazy looking for her, and there were so many people, I didn't even know where to look. And you were waiting to take me home. And we walked and walked through the slush and the mud, and people were hurrying all around us and . . . and . . .

" 'But this part is sad. All of a sudden I saw Little Sheba. She was lying in the middle of the field . . . dead. It make me cry, Doc. No one paid any attention . . . I cried and cried. It make me feel so bad, Doc. That sweet little puppy . . . her curly white fur all smeared with mud, and no one to stop and take care of her . . .

" 'You kept saying, "We can't stay here, honey, we gotta go on. We gotta go on." Now, isn't that strange?

" 'I don't think Little Sheba's ever coming back, Doc. I'm not going to call her anymore . . .

" 'I'll fix your eggs.' "

Otis recognized it, all right. It was the most famous scene from William Inge's play *Come Back, Little Sheba.* Shirley Booth had played the part in the movie—the character's name was Lola—and spoken those words to Burt Lancaster, who had played Doc.

He wanted to tell Sally that she was as good a Shirley Booth—and prettier, even—as he was a Johnny Mercer.

In a sudden burst of new emotion, Sally started sobbing again. She said through her tears, "I'm sorry, Otis. I am so, so sorry. Please forgive me. Please, please, forgive me."

Otis had no idea what she was talking about. Forgive you for not being Shirley Booth? That didn't make sense. Forgive you for reciting that Inge scene? No way it could be that. Forgive you for what?

She must be talking about something else. But what? What had she done to apologize to *him* for? Maybe she was sorry she waited until after Annabel and Josh Garnett to really come talk to him after the accident.

I forgive you, Sally!

He wanted to tell her that, and that she was as good as Shirley Booth.

But Otis wasn't sure he was going to speak any more words. Or show any more real progress. He had, under the cover of darkness, begun to move around a bit. Nobody knew about it. And maybe that's the way it would be, at least for a while.

Until Buck figured out exactly what he was going to do next—besides sing.

THIRTEEN

ONE OF HIS first singing triumphs, appropriately enough, got him some chocolate fudge.

Through the careful use of frowns, smiles, nods, and head shakes, he had been able to order one of his favorite meals: a cheeseburger with fried onions and a Dr Pepper to drink.

The attendant asked if there was anything else he would like, a special treat of some kind.

Otis replied with a musical outburst that sent the message that he wanted something sweet.

After several minutes, a Butterfinger was brought to Otis and placed in his right hand. He didn't take hold of it. One after another at varying intervals, he also didn't grab a Milky Way or a Baby Ruth or a Reese's peanut butter cup or a Heath bar or a peanut cluster or a Tootsie Roll or a Hershey's Kiss or a chocolate-covered mint patty or a chewy caramel square or a lemon drop or a peppermint stick.

Then a two-inch square of chocolate fudge was placed in his right hand. He folded his hands around the candy and brought it to his mouth.

"Eureka! As we say here in Eureka," said somebody male in the room. Otis's vision was clearing up. He could have looked, but he didn't want to. It was probably Tonganoxie. It was the kind of thing he'd say.

Otis quickly accepted and ate two pieces of fudge despite his modest disappointment with the quality and taste. It was commercially made, smooth and milky, but not as grainy soft as Otis's grandmother's or Church Key's.

Church Key Something Blue. It had been a while since Otis had thought about that idiot—that shithead. For a few minutes Otis considered the possibility of Church Key's having been part of a dream or part of a hallucination that had been brought on by the near-drowning in the Chanute River. But the timing didn't add up. Otis was sure he'd had the experience with that idiot, that shithead, before the Cushman crashed through the bridge. Yes, that was right. Church Key was real. Otis considered how many other idiots—morons, lunatics, numbskulls, and shitheads—there could be out there making fudge or stealing money from people on motor scooters or doing other crazy or bad things. Do former professional football players all go a bit nuts and mean once their playing days are over?

What about singers and songwriters? Did Johnny Mercer stay cool and sane and with it until he died in 1976? What a year to die! Our bicentennial year. Otis remembered the obituary in the *Eureka Times.* "Johnny Mercer, the songwriter and singer from Georgia they called Our Huckleberry Friend from his song 'Moon River,' died yesterday of a brain tumor in Bel Air, California, at the age of 67."

Poor Johnny, poor Johnny, how could you die? Poor Johnny, poor Johnny, oh.

After chewing and swallowing a third piece of fudge, poor Otis sang:

"Gather 'round me everybody
Gather 'round me
While I preach some.
Feel a sermon comin' on me
The topic will be sin
And that's what I'm a-gin.
If you wanna hear my story
Then settle back and just sit tight
While I start reviewin'
The attitude of doin' right.
You've got to ac-cent-tchu-ate the positive
Eliminate the negative,
Latch on to the affirmative
Don't mess with Mister In-between.
You've got to spread joy up to the maximum
Bring gloom down to the minimum
Have faith or pandemonium
Li'ble to walk upon the scene."

Otis stopped, accepted another piece of fudge, and ate it.

"I recognize that song from something," said a female in the room. It wasn't Sally or the non-Sharon nurse. It must be another nurse or female doctor or rehab assistant. Or somebody just passing by. Again Otis chose not to appear to care. All in good time. *His* good time.

"I think it was in that *Midnight in the Garden of Good and Evil* movie down in Georgia," said another woman, who also did not sound familiar.

Johnny was from Savannah! That's why it was in the movie! You idiot!

Otis picked up the song:

"To illustrate my last remark:
Jonah in the whale,
Noah in the ark.
What did they do
Just when everything looked so dark?
Man, they said we'd better
Ac-cent-tchu-ate the positive,
Eliminate the negative,
Latch on to the affirmative
Don't mess with Mister In-between."

Otis stopped singing and listened to the applause of the people in the room he had chosen not to see.

THERE WAS AN outburst from "That Old Black Magic." It came in response to a male nursing attendant who, as someone did every morning, was giving Otis a bath in the hospital bed. Otis had graduated from tubes that took away his various wastes to a bedpan, although, unbeknownst to anyone, he was able to go to the bathroom on his own as well as wash himself.

His minders and doctors would find out, all in *his* good time.

The attendant, who Otis believed was named Bud, said as he put a hot washcloth on Otis's back, "Now, how does that feel this morning, Mr. Halstead?"

Otis sang:

"That old black magic has me in its spell.
That old black magic that you weave so well.
Those icy fingers up and down my spine . . ."

Within seconds, several other people were in the room listening to Otis. He didn't look at them, but he knew they

were there. They stayed to applaud when he finished with
the lines:

"The same old tingle that I feel inside
And then that elevator starts its ride
And down and down I go,
'Round and 'round I go
Like a leaf that's caught in the tide."

Bud was a black man, but that had nothing to do with Otis's
choosing the song. He hoped Bud understood and was not
offended and did not think Otis was a racist. Otis remembered
a race-sensitivity class he and the other executives at KCF&C
had attended a while ago. The instructor had said all white people should assume that all black people they met thought all
white people were racists. It struck Otis as a stupid way of
thinking, but it stuck with him. He couldn't get the assumption
out of his mind every time he met or talked to a black person,
even one named Bud who was bathing him in a hospital bed.

Later, a female nutritionist said to him that for supper, he
might try something else for dessert besides chocolate fudge.
Otis had already imagined serious meetings by Drs. Severy and
Tonganoxie and others to contemplate why Otis Halstead
seemed obsessed with chocolate fudge. Was there a serious fudge
event in his childhood? Maybe an uncle he hated had choked to
death on chocolate fudge?

Otis's response to the nutritionist was four lines of the Mercer
tune "Hooray for Spinach," from a movie called *Naughty but
Nice.*

"Hooray for spinach!
Hooray for milk!

They put the roses in your cheek soft as silk,
They helped complete you till I could meet you, baby!"

Within minutes, Otis had a plate of spinach before him. He frowned until it was taken away. Then they brought him a small bowl of mashed spinach, which he also frowned away.

Then came a glass of milk, which he sipped dry through a straw.

He burped loudly to a round of clapping.

The next day he sang from the same song:

"Hooray for sunshine!
Hooray for air!
They put the permanent in your curly hair,
They helped to raise you till I could praise you, baby."

That was what led to Otis going outside for the first time since arriving at the Ashland Clinic.

Several people picked him up from his bed and sat him down in a wheelchair. They had no idea he could walk on his own. He also acted as if he couldn't keep his head up straight, so they strapped it loosely against the back of the chair, the same way they did his chest, stomach, arms, and legs. No need to rush things.

It was a nice day outside. A nice spring day. That clearly wasn't a Christmas decoration he'd seen on the ceiling. Must have been an illusion—a mirage. Or something else. Well, there's the sun up there, and the sky is Kansas blue, and the clouds are white. Good for all of them. Everything is where it should be, looking the way it should look here in the Sunflower State.

And the air feels good. Hooray for air! Let's hear it, Johnny Our Huckleberry Friend!

Otis sang, "Hooray for sunshine! Hooray for air!"
Then the second verse of "Sunflower."

"Skies are fair in Kansas,
Clouds are rare in Kansas,
Never saw a place that could
Compare with Kansas . . ."

They rolled him to what appeared to be a patio, not unlike his patio in Eureka that was called an outdoor entertainment area. Here there was also something hard and gray, like concrete or slate, and there were big cottonwoods and sycamores all around. *Anybody have a spare Red Ryder BB gun?*
Several people were sitting in chairs in a semicircle facing him. He recognized three of them: Madison Severy, Russ Tonganoxie the shithead, and Bob Gidney. This must be something important, for the three of them to be here. He tried to make eye contact with each of them one at a time, as a way of saying hello—also of giving them a progress event to discuss. There was another man and a woman sitting across from him, but he did not recognize them, so he did not lock eyes with them. *I'm Buck the scooter man. Who are you?*
Too bad Johnny Mercer died. Boy, could he have written a great song called "Scooter Man." It could be the fun-filled Huckleberry Friend kind of story about a bald-headed blood-sucking insurance executive who headed west on a 1952 Cushman Pacemaker, fell through a condemned bridge, and instead of drowning, became a singer just like Johnny Mercer.
"We think you can talk," said Bob Gidney, "as well as look at us straight in the eye, as you did just now."
"You're playing games with us, aren't you, Otis?" said the shithead Russ Tonganoxie.

"I feel strongly, Otis, that the words are there for you to speak, and all it takes is for you to decide to speak them," said Mad Severy. "You spoke one—'Sharon.' You can speak others."

Bob Gidney said, "These other two people with us are Drs. Ruth Humboldt and Clay F. Sublette. They're psychiatric colleagues of ours from the University of Washington School of Medicine in Seattle."

Otis moved his eyes toward the pair. *What does the F stand for?* was the only question he could think of to ask, if he were in the business of asking questions. I met a great young man whose name was T. He came to see me at the clinic, but Mad wouldn't let him in. T spelled his name without a period, à la Harry S Truman. Is your F with or without a period, Doctor?

Bob Gidney continued, "Drs. Humboldt and Sublette have done a lot of work with the mental rehabilitation of near-drowning victims. But they have never encountered—personally or in the literature—any cases like yours."

Dr. Sublette said, "That's right, Mr. Halstead. No one has ever substituted singing for speaking the way you have. If people can sing, they can also talk. That is true even for those recovering from trauma, as you are."

"Singing mostly one particular songwriter's songs makes it even more unusual," said Dr. Humboldt. "Our research on the issue is clear—it has never happened before."

"Not only with near-drowning victims, Mr. Halstead," said Dr. Sublette, "but not with any other kind of stroke or other victims left with a mental-function impairment of some kind."

"That's why we think you're faking it," said Tonganoxie the shithead.

Bob Gidney said, "No need to get rough, Russ."

"A man who can sing a Johnny Mercer song can talk," Tonganoxie responded. "You know it and I know it and they know it and everybody in the world knows it. You don't have to be a shrink to know it."

"Don't use the word 'shrink,' " Bob Gidney said. "That's self-hate offensive."

"This whole thing is offensive," said Madison Severy. "This is obviously a sick man who needs treatment, not childish fights between his doctors."

Wrong! A childish fight was exactly what he needed, thought Otis. *Sic 'em! Fight, fight, fight! Great, great, great!*

Ignoring the shrink controversy, Dr. Sublette said to Otis, "We would like to ask you some questions, if we might. We would clearly hope and prefer that you answer them—the old-fashioned way, if you will—with words, but we have composed them in such a way that moving your head slightly in a nod for yes and a shake for no will suffice. Is the strap on your head loose enough for you to respond that way? If so, please nod. If not, please shake."

Otis nodded.

Drs. Humboldt and Sublette alternated asking questions. Sublette went first. "Our research indicates that Johnny Mercer wrote more than one thousand songs—one thousand two hundred and twelve, to be exact—that were published. Does that coincide with your information, Mr. Halstead?"

Otis nodded.

"Do you know the words to all twelve hundred and twelve?"

Otis shook his head slightly.

"More than half?"

After a pause of a few seconds, Otis shook again.

"Less than half?"

A shake.

"About half?"

Nod.

"So that means you know the words to some six hundred Johnny Mercer songs. Is that right?"

Nod.

"You're lying, Otis," said Tonganoxie. "Nobody in the world knows the words to six hundred of any kind of songs."

Otis did not move his head.

"Is it correct that you learned the songs—no matter the exact number—when you were young?" Dr. Sublette continued.

Nod.

"In high school or before?"

Nod and shake.

"You mean you learned some of them in high school or before, and some of them afterward?"

Nod.

"Mrs. Halstead has told us that she had no knowledge of your ability to sing Mercer songs, or to sing at all, until your recent accident. Have you sung many Mercer songs in the last thirty-five years?"

Shake.

"Since high school?"

Shake.

"So you stopped singing like Johnny Mercer or any other way after high school?"

Nod.

"Did something happen—a specific event—that caused you to stop singing?"

Otis kept his head absolutely still.

"Did you hear the question, Mr. Halstead?"

Nod.

"But you're not going to answer it, is that it?"

Nod.

"Why not, goddammit?" Russ Tonganoxie yelled.

"Cool it, Russ," Bob Gidney said. "For whatever reason, he's not going to answer the question. We'll have to find out ourselves."

"I think we are in the process of discovering a completely new syndrome," said Dr. Sublette.

"I agree," said Dr. Humboldt.

Tonganoxie, in a state of high sneer, said, "Oh, sure. Eureka! What shall we call it? The Johnny Mercer syndrome? The Halstead syndrome? Or why not simply Otis? A disease named Otis. Every time we come across somebody who only sings Mercer songs instead of talking—I'm sure there are millions of the poor souls out there, waiting to be found and helped—we'll stroke our beards and lower our Viennese accents and say, 'Dear patient, you have Otis and, so sorry to report, there is no cure for Otis. You will sing Johnny Mercer songs instead of talking for the rest of your life.' "

Otis listened for laughter. There was none. Not even a slight giggle. Otis would have been delighted to laugh out loud and uproariously if he had decided to do that sort of thing. Not yet.

Russ Tonganoxie may not be a shithead after all.

Bob Gidney said to Otis, "What would you like to do now?"

Otis sang from Johnny's 1942 song "Hit the Road to Dreamland":

"Bye-bye, baby,
Time to hit the road to dreamland.
Don't cry, baby . . .
Time to hit the road."

Russ Tonganoxie cackled with laughter.

"He wants a nap, he's tired," said Dr. Sublette. He and the others were not laughing, because they were clearly unhappy.

And sad and worried and concerned. That was the way they looked to Otis, at least. Finally, Bob Gidney confirmed it.

"If we don't come up with something, this poor man—my friend Otis Halstead—is going to live the rest of his life this way, answering questions with Johnny Mercer songs instead of spoken words," he said. "We must do everything in our power to bring him back to his old self, his old life, his old happiness."

Drs. Sublette and Humboldt said in unison, "We will do our best, Bob."

"You know what I think," said Russ Tonganoxie. "I think this man Otis Halstead has absolutely no interest in being brought back to his old life—his old happiness."

Nod.

"You found it, Otis, you found it, didn't you?" Tonganoxie asked.

Nod.

"Eureka. You're yelling Eureka, aren't you, Otis?"

Otis yelled at the top of his lungs: "Eureka!"

He decided there was no harm in giving them another word—another small progress event—to ponder and to confuse.

While Buck prepared to make his move.

FOURTEEN

RUSS TONGANOXIE, AS always at patient assessment staff meetings about Otis, cracked jokes.

"Why don't we make some tapes and CDs of Otis's singing and market them to music lovers the world over? 'Otis Sings Mercer.' We could even create our own label. 'Ashland Rocks.' Or 'Schizo Songs'? 'Crazy Rhythms'? We could make some money, pave the parking lot, expand the cafeteria."

Nobody laughed. Nobody had any optimistic assessments or new treatment ideas for Otis, either.

On the way out of the conference room a few minutes later, Russ Tonganoxie surprised Bob Gidney by suggesting they have lunch together. They quickly agreed on the Turkey Red Café, a onetime wheat farm outside town that had been converted into the Eureka area's best and most popular restaurant.

Russ and Bob had yet to develop anything other than a working relationship. That was why the invitation surprised Bob.

They rode in Russ's shiny, sporty sand-colored Jeep Wrangler. The Jeep's canvas top was in place, but it was open on both sides because it was a warm day, and Russ had removed the side doors and windows.

"We'll start with a vodka martini, on the rocks with two olives," said Russ.

"No way, no thanks," said Bob.

But immediately after they were seated at a private corner table at the restaurant, Russ ordered a martini for each of them from a young waitress. She was dressed in a long cotton dress with a white pinafore that matched the decor.

There was real hay up in the loft of the onetime barn, a restored 1938 Ford tractor and plow displayed like pieces of sculpture over by the bar, old scythes, rakes, and other hand implements along with farm scene photos and oil paintings on the walls.

A casual observer would have had trouble guessing Russ and Bob had enough in common to share even a meal. Both were dressed in their usual manner. Russ Tonganoxie was in faded blue jeans, white sneakers, and a wrinkled long-sleeved blue-and-white-striped polo shirt. Bob Gidney was wearing tasseled black loafers, a sharply pressed dark blue hopsack suit, a blue oxford button-down, and a wine silk tie. Russ's hair was mostly uncombed, while every strand of Bob's seemed freshly fixed.

After a few minutes, the martinis were delivered. Russ grabbed his and raised it. Bob just looked at his and said, "I haven't had a real martini in years. They make me drunk and sometimes giddy, sometimes teary."

"Pick it up," Russ said. "At least let's have a clink."

"I have several appointments this afternoon," said Bob. But he did raise his glass and knock it against Russ's.

"So do I. But right now I want to talk about you. I have watched you sliding down some kind of slippery slope since Otis's accident. I understand your friendship, but I sense there's something more, something deeper, going on. Am I right?"

Bob took a sip of his martini. He said, "Sure. I hadn't realized it was so obvious."

"You've lost your spark, your verve, your involvement, your engagement. You seem distracted, mostly somewhere else."

"I wish I were mostly somewhere else."

"Where?"

"Anywhere else."

Both Russ and Bob ordered the Country Sampler lunch special—a large plate that included a crisp-fried chicken breast, a small slice of sugared baked ham, a three-inch piece of buttered corn on the cob, separate spoonfuls of slightly cooked green beans and black-eyed peas, a splat of onion-flavored mashed potatoes, a thick slice of ripe tomato, and three radishes. Everything had been raised there on the farm. On the side came gigantic glasses of iced tea, a basket of warm wheat biscuits and corn-bread sticks, and freshly whipped butter served in a fruit-preserves jar.

Russ noticed that Bob took a second and then a third sip of his martini.

"Have you talked to anybody about what's going on with you?" Russ asked.

"No."

"Why not?"

Bob took his fourth sip. Russ covertly signaled to the waitress for two more martinis.

"It's not ripe for talking," said Bob. "I feel guilty about some things concerning Otis, that's all. It'll pass. If it gets to a point where I need to talk to you or somebody else, I'll let you know. And relax. I am not about to kill myself . . . Sorry, Russ."

Russ shook his head but said nothing.

Without comment or apparent notice, Bob soon was several sips into his second martini. So was Russ.

They idly talked awhile about the restaurant and Eureka and Kansas, as well as the clinic and a few new psychiatric studies that intrigued one or the other. Russ told Bob that something interesting had turned up on Canton, the deputy sheriff who had saved Otis's life and then died himself. It turned out that he was a Silver Star.

"He claimed he had been a motorcycle cop in Wichita and that he had been hurt in an accident there. Not so. He spent his whole life working on farms out near the Colorado border. Nobody checked out his references when they hired him as a deputy because they liked him, he told good stories about his motorcycle days, and they happened to need somebody in a hurry."

"I thought the sheriff said he was the best deputy they ever had," Bob said.

"He still says that. Very common for Silver Stars. In order to keep their fantasy lie going, they have to be better than anybody else."

Bob left for the men's room. While he was gone, Russ used his cellphone to call the clinic. He told his secretary to cancel his afternoon appointments and to pass on the message to Dr. Gidney's secretary to do the same.

When Bob returned, Russ asked, "Do you still get a kick out of psychiatry, Bob?"

"Oh, please, for God's sake. I'm not interested in being one of your mature-male-in-crisis subjects."

Russ grinned, looked away, and then pressed on.

"I hit on Otis about being a bloodsucking insurance man. He hit back, calling us brainsuckers. Maybe he's right. We live off the troubled minds and souls of humankind. It certainly bothers me sometimes, I must confess. I understand also why Otis Halstead wanted to run away. God knows I have certainly had that desire more than once. My work really does bear out that running away is one of the most common of desires among well-educated professionals. I would assume that you've had your runaway moments, too."

"Shut up, Russ. Okay?"

Their food arrived with two more martinis.

"What did you do that made you feel so guilty about Otis?" Russ asked after a couple of minutes.

Bob, in a vodka-soaked monotone, said, "I've always tried to control my own life. I believe in conserving my mental and physical energy for things that matter to me. I talk only when I want to talk and only about what I want to talk about, when I want to talk about it. My guilt feelings about Otis, if they exist, are not on the list at this particular moment at the Turkey Red Café—"

"Fine," Russ interrupted. "But if you feel guilty for not having helped Otis through his running-away crisis, forget it. I may have been the one who planted the idea of running away on the motor scooter."

"You? When?"

"When he and I talked that first and only time at the clinic. We were talking about the scooter, and I said something flip, something smart-ass—my style—about a motor scooter not being very good for running away from home. I even advised him to stay off the interstates, which he did, and fell into a river for his trouble."

"Well, I gave him the idea for the Cushman. We were talking about his BB gun and his toy fire engine. He asked me if there was anything I ever wanted that I couldn't have, and I said a red Cushman. He said him, too. And he went off to Nebraska and bought one. If I hadn't planted the idea of the Cushman in his troubled head, he might not have run away, and you know the rest."

"Might, might, might. The three most powerful words in the

rationalizing of human behavior." Russ closed his eyes and leaned back in his chair.

The waitress arrived as they finished their meal and gave them the choice of peach, cherry, or blueberry cobbler served warm under a slice of melting Colby cheese and a gob of home-made vanilla ice cream. Russ chose cherry, Bob peach.

"Planting the Cushman idea doesn't work for me as a cause for your being in such a guilt fuck—funk, sorry," Russ said after the desserts were delivered. "The scooter was a vehicle, in more ways than one, but that's all it was. If he hadn't had that, he would have used or done something else. You know that. Sorry, Bob, but I'm not buying. There's got to be more going on."

"I'm having an affair with Sally Halstead."

Bob said it suddenly and quietly, with his face down in his cobbler. Russ wasn't sure he had heard what he thought he had heard.

"Did you say what I hope I did not hear you say?"

"Yes. That is what I feel guilty about. He was—is—one of my best friends. A real friend, under my definition. She—Sally—was—is—one of my wife's best friends. And there it was. Sally came to me at the clinic to talk about Otis's back-to-childhood problems, and in the course of those conversations, we found ourselves . . . well, in compromising positions. I hate it. I hate myself. I cannot stand it. I was about to stop it and maybe even tell Otis when he ran away on that goddamn motor scooter."

"Don't tell him now, okay?"

"Goddamn, Russ! What kind of fool do you think I am? There is no way I would do something like that. It could kill him."

Russ Tonganoxie was smiling and shaking his head. He put his napkin to his mouth. "I doubt that."

"Are you sick?" Bob asked.

"Not yet. I'm just trying to keep from breaking up."

"This is not funny, you idiot. What's wrong with you? Get a grip. Maybe everything Woody Allen and the great lay world think about us is right. Maybe we're all crazier than our patients are."

"I was just thinking about the scene. You go into Otis's room at the clinic. You confess to having an affair with his wife. And what happens? He breaks into a Johnny Mercer song."

Bob Gidney turned his head away in disgust. Then he started laughing himself. "Did Mercer write a song about adultery?"

"I'm sure he did, I'm sure he did. We'll check it on the Internet."

"Oh, come on. Not Our Huckleberry Friend."

Russ stopped laughing. "Hey, what was Mercer's famous blues song?"

" 'Blues in the Night'?"

"Yeah. According to Otis's daily nurses' chart, he sang part of it the other night. How does it go?"

"Something like 'My momma done told me . . .' "

"Right. 'When I was in knee pants . . .' "

" 'My momma done told me . . .' "

" 'Son.' "

" 'A woman'll sweet-talk . . .' "

" 'And give ya the big eye . . .' "

" 'But when the sweet talkin's done . . .' "

In unison, they sang:

" 'A woman's a two-faced
Worrisome thing who'll leave ya t'sing
The blu-uues in the night.' "

They applauded themselves and looked around to see if anyone in the restaurant was paying attention. Nobody was. Long martini lunches were definitely not the rule in Eureka, Kansas. The other customers were gone, and the staff was busy cleaning up and setting the tables for dinner.

"Maybe we could do a CD for the Crazy Rhythms label," Russ said. "Bob and Russ, the Singing Shrinks."

Bob Gidney did not raise his usual objection to the term "shrink." He was too busy sobbing violently into his hands, which were cupped together in front of his lowered, shaking, reddened face.

Russ let him cry. As a matter of professional belief and personal practice, Russ supported a good cry as a legitimate form of therapy. Kept-in, spontaneous emotion of any kind can breed mental unrest and disaster, was his theory, one shared by many others in his field.

He was about to say something comforting to Bob to that effect—something such as "Let the tears flow, Bob"—when the cellphone in his right pants pocket sounded.

Russ listened for only a couple of seconds before standing up and saying into the phone, "We're on our way."

To Bob Gidney, he said, "Otis has run away. He just put on his clothes and walked out."

RUSS DID NOT feel the aftereffects of his martini lunch until that evening, when he turned down the street to his home. Nervous energy and the stimulation of dealing with Otis's disappearance had not only masked any drunkenness earlier, they had held back a hangover later.

But now it hit him in a rush. His mouth, his stomach, his brain seemed overstuffed with vomit and garbage and trash.

He pulled the Wrangler into his driveway and drove straight for the large garage in back.

In virtually one continuous motion, he braked to a stop and leaned out of the Jeep far to the left.

God bless you, my sweet little Jeep. No doors or windows to deal with. Perfect for barfing, absolutely perfect.

Everything he had eaten and drunk—for days or weeks or months, it seemed—came rushing into and through his mouth. When it finally ran out, he continued to heave for several more minutes until there wasn't even a drop of sour spit left.

"You okay?" somebody asked. It was a male voice. A vaguely familiar male voice. Whoever it belonged to was standing in a shadow. There were lights back here, but also some dark spots where the light didn't shine.

Great, thought Russ. *A perfect ending to this lousy goddamned day. Now I'm going to be robbed. Here in the Sunflower State, here at my new home on the range where the buffalo roam, the deer and the antelope play, and the skies are not cloudy all day, here in the Land of Oz, where Judy Garland and Bert Lahr and Jack Haley walked the Yellow Brick Road in no fear.*

"What do you want?" he said into the darkness. "Whatever it is, take it and get out of here. I'm sick as hell, and I need to go to bed."

"I want one of your Jeeps."

"You sound familiar. I know you, don't I? Come out into the light, for chrissake. If you're going to hijack a Jeep, have the criminal balls to do it out in the open."

The man stepped into the light about ten yards away. It was Otis Halstead. "Eureka," Otis said quietly.

"Eureka, my ass!" said Russ in as loud and angry a shout as his condition would permit. "You singing vegetable asshole! I was right about you playing possum!" Russ slid out of the seat, being careful not to step in the puddle of his vomit on the driveway. "Where are you headed?"

"West. Same as before."

"Got a big sixtieth-birthday blowout planned?"

Otis only smiled.

Russ Tonganoxie did not see himself as a strong or tough guy, but clearly, even in his barfy condition, he could handle Otis. They were about the same stature and muscle size—medium to small, average to weak—but Otis had been mostly in bed for the last several days. That meant he was even weaker than usual. Unless Otis had a weapon of some kind, no problem. A weapon was not likely, unless he had picked up another Red Ryder BB gun somewhere.

"I'm not giving you the keys to this Jeep or any of the others—they're antiques," Russ said. "You're going to have to take them from me by force, and I plan to resist with every ounce of energy I have."

He didn't feel sick or tired anymore. He was professionally aroused, curious, ready. This could be fun.

He walked right at Otis, who was dressed in a long-sleeved red-and-white-checked button-down, khaki slacks, and slippers.

"I paid nineteen thousand eight hundred and fifty-seven dollars for this Wrangler," Russ said as he approached Otis. "It's top-of-the-line. Soft top and removable side-door curtains for good weather, like now. Hard top for cold weather. Four-wheel drive. Five-speed manual transmission. Four-point-oh-liter, six-cylinder engine. P-225/75-R-15 Goodyear tires—"

"I'll get you twenty thousand even plus another two thousand—a kind of service charge for wear and tear—as soon as I can. My word is good."

Russ stopped two yards from Otis, who had made no sign of moving. He was standing his ground.

"Your word sucks, Otis," said Russ. "You jerk us around and play games with us, acting as if you're mostly out of it, capable of only singing like Johnny Mercer." Changing to a mocking, sneering, half-singing voice, he shimmied, shook his shoulders à la Elvis and said, " 'Do yuh hear that engine down the line? I figure that it's engine number forty-nine.' What crap that was. Suckers. You played us for suckers. And you and your word suck."

Russ turned toward the door of his large garage. He pointed a small electronic device at the door, and it came up, turning on lights and thus illuminating his three other Jeeps inside.

Otis followed Russ into the garage. "Tell me about the Jeeps, Russ." They were lined up in military formation, not unlike the Cushman King's scooters up in Nebraska. One hundred and thirty-four and counting.

"That first one there on the left is the real *real* World War Two McCoy," said Russ. "It's got the shovel on the side and the extra gas can on the back, as you can see. The windshield folds down. The whole thing weighs only eighteen hundred pounds. Anybody could push it out of a ditch. I bought it from the son of a guy who took it with him when he got out of the army after the war—stole the damned thing, for all I know.

"The next one—the red thing of beauty—is the Jeepster convertible. Slightly longer than the original Jeep. Look at the whitewalls, the chrome on the front. A Jeep, but something very special.

"Then my little red-white-and-blue right-hand-drive postal Jeep. Police also used them for parking-meter duty."

"How did you get them out here from the East Coast?"

"I drove one out with another hooked behind on a trailer hitch. Then I flew back and got the other two and drove them out the same way. I took different routes each time—both were great trips, one across on I-70 through Columbus and Indianapolis and Kansas City. The other, longer but prettier, on the old U.S. 50

through the West Virginia mountains, Cincinnati, Vincennes, Indiana."

"You're as nuts as I am, you know."

Russ said nothing and went on toward the far door that led into the house.

Otis said, "Help me, Russ. Playing dumb and out of it, as I've been doing, is punishment enough."

Russ waved him off, walked on, opened the outside and screen doors, and disappeared inside the house.

"If I still had my Red Ryder BB gun, I'd shoot the lights out on all these Jeeps of yours!" Otis shouted after him.

Russ stuck his head out from behind the screen door. "Get your crazy Red Ryder ass in here, and let's talk about all of this."

"You're crazier than I am! Jeeps, motor scooters, what's the difference?"

"The number of wheels! Jeeps have four, motor scooters have two!"

"Mercer wrote a Jeeps song." Otis did a little two-step movement with his feet and sang:

"*Jeep*ers, creepers,
Where'd ya get those peepers?
Jeepers, creepers,
Where'd ya get those eyes?"

Soon Otis and Russ were sitting on stools across from each other at the butcher-block top of a high kitchen table. Otis was talking.

"I started getting better almost from the beginning. I hid it from Mad Severy and everybody else. At the very start, I really was unable to see anybody clearly, to move or talk—that's really true. But I had my hearing and my wits about me. And slowly,

my vision came back, and I said my one glorious word—
'Sharon.' Then 'Eureka!'—that was for you."

"Thanks a lot. Sharon. I want to know about her."

"There's nothing to know except an unreal fantasy and a real
wet dream."

Russ offered to get Otis something to eat or drink. Otis
passed and simply kept talking while Russ poured himself a
glass of Diet Coke over ice; his stomach took a pass on anything
else.

"I started singing. All the words to the old Mercer tunes came
back to me like I had just learned them. I don't know how or
why; they just did. You were right when you said I had no desire
to return to the life I had run away from."

Russ told Otis how they had turned his problem into an official syndrome, one he wanted to call simply "Otis." He said he
should call Mad Severy or somebody at the clinic right now and
tell them Otis the Escaped Singer had been found.

No way, said Otis. "They'll all come over here and try to keep
me from running away again. One of the reasons I played possum games was because I didn't want to recover right back into
my old life. I've led a deadened life for fifty-nine years—almost
sixty—and deadened everyone else's around me. My family's, my
colleagues'. Look what I did to Pete Wetmore. You call and I go.
I'll literally run away on my own two feet if you won't give me
a Jeep."

Russ nodded, making no move toward a phone, and asked
when Otis had felt really recovered, when and how he had realized he could talk and get up out of bed, walk, and move around.

Otis said, "When I was alone, I spoke only to myself. I had to
be careful when I talked, so I spoke quietly, sometimes even in a
whisper. At first it was mostly about sneaking to the bathroom.
I had to get in and out of there quickly, when I was pretty sure

no nurse or attendant or one of you hotshots was due to visit. I had to learn to leave a little for the bedpan or somebody might wonder why I could go so long without."

Russ wanted to know how he'd gotten away from the clinic and over here in slippers. They had determined that there was only a set of sport clothes in Otis's closet. No shoes.

"Hitchhiked. First ride was with a guy delivering bottled water. The second with a Sears catalog credit checker. He had a phone book in his car, and I looked up your address. He dropped me four blocks from here." Otis stepped down from his stool.

Russ looked at his wristwatch and then, for good measure, at a large round clock over his refrigerator. "It's almost nine o'clock, and it's dark as hell out there. This is a stupid time to set out."

Otis began moving slowly toward the door to the garage.

Russ leaped off his stool and cut Otis off, blocking his way. They ended up under a yard apart.

"Don't screw with me, Russ. This is my life, my Eureka, we're talking about here."

"I had an idea about recording you singing some of the Mercer songs. Call it *Otis Sings Mercer,* something like that. You could finally be what you always wanted to be."

Otis shook his head. "You're playing with me, and it won't work. Get out of the way."

Russ sprang into a boxer's crouch. "You're going to have to punch me out of the way, fella." He said it in a tone and accent that vaguely resembled that of an Italian mobster.

Otis took a large, forceful step to his left—Russ's right—and Russ made no move to stop him. "Okay, you win." Russ reached into his pants pocket and pulled out some keys, pulled one off a ring, and tossed it to Otis. "Take the Wrangler. Can you drive a stick shift?"

A look of wonder and joy came across Otis's face. "You're a good man, Russ Tonganoxie. Even if you're a little wacko. You might want to talk to somebody sometime about your Jeep problem. There must be somebody at Ashland who specializes in treating people who love Jeeps. Yeah, it's been a while, but I can do stick shift."

"I'm going with you."

"What?"

"I'm going to run away, too. I hate this place and everything about it. My brainsucking job sucks. I talk to one guy, Pete Wetmore, and he kills himself. I talk to another—you—and he runs away from home on a motor scooter. Give me a minute to throw some things in a bag. What about money?"

"I have my MasterCard. They left it with my driver's license on a shelf in the closet. I'll stop at an ATM somewhere."

"Me, too, then."

"What about the other Jeeps?"

"I'll drive one of them—the old army Jeep. I'll just leave the other two here for somebody to dispose of. I'll call Gidney or somebody from the road. They can sell the house, too, and every-thing in it, and send me a check."

Russ disappeared down a hallway to his bedroom to throw some clothes and a shaving kit into a suitcase. Within a few minutes, he heard the sound of the Wrangler's motor outside.

He raced back to the kitchen and to an outside door.

The Wrangler and Otis were gone.

The only sign of them was a handwritten note Otis had left under Russ's glass of Diet Coke on the kitchen table.

Russ—

I'll run away my way and you run yours. I think you want to go the other direction anyhow—back toward the East, where you really live. Wherever you go, I'll eventually find you and get you the money for the Jeep. I'll take good care of it. Please don't tell anybody you saw me and what I'm driving. I need some time to get really away this time. Thanks. Eureka.

Otis

—By the way, you called it right at the beginning.
I'm a classic No Need Monster.

Russ Tonganoxie had never been as full of conflicted thoughts and drives and instincts and desires as he was at this moment.

He could jump in the Fort Benning Jeep and go west after Otis—or go back east.

He could call the police and report his Wrangler stolen by Otis Halstead.

He could call Sally Halstead and tell her that Otis was safe but gone west again.

He could do what Otis had asked—call no one, do nothing, give him a day or two to get lost.

He could carefully parse the emotional words he'd spoken a few minutes ago about hating this place and his job.

He could begin wondering whether he really would have run away with Otis Halstead. Or was it an unconscious professional trick aimed at keeping Otis under supervision, under care, under treatment?

He could just go to bed and try to sleep everything off.

And that was what he did.

His main regret was that he hadn't asked Otis if he really did know the words to six hundred Johnny Mercer songs.

FIFTEEN

OTIS, MEANWHILE, WAS approaching the home and fudge factory of Church Key Charlie Blue.

It presented Otis with the delightful temptation to pause briefly for a second hit of retribution. Despite his BB-gun revenge, he was still most annoyed at what the shithead jerk had done to him. It should have been long gone and far away from his mind—and throat—by now, but it wasn't.

Onward, Buck.

Otis did slow down. He saw a flickering light from the television in the home half of Church Key Charlie Blue's ratty place. Charlie couldn't be watching a football game, because it wasn't Sunday or Monday. What are you watching, Charlie? *Booknotes* on C-SPAN? An A&E documentary on the Cold War?

How about a two-hour PBS special on Archimedes?

Do you still have my four thou in your helmet, Charlie?

Otis slowed the Jeep so much that he had to hit the clutch and thrust the gear shift into second. There was some lurching and grinding, but he did it. He was already getting better at shifting. It was coming back. And he loved it. There was something about using a stick shift that gave the driver control of the vehicle. A human being had to do more than just get in, turn on the ignition, put it in D, and drive off. Driving required skill and practice and even some active thinking on occasion.

The Ford pickup, the one his dad had driven in front of the Santa Fe freight, had been a stick shift. Was he trying to beat that train in third gear, or had he shifted it down to second for power?

Minutes after he'd screeched away from Tonganoxie's house, Otis had a genuine feel for why Russ liked Jeeps, even this tony Wrangler model. They seemed close to the road, real, unaffected. Otis had kept the speed up there, at least fifty most of the time. He wanted to get away, to get west, as soon as possible.

He discounted the possibility that Russ Tonganoxie might sic the police on him. Russ wouldn't do that. Russ Tonganoxie was neither an idiot nor a shithead. He was a good man, as good as Bob Gidney, in his own way. Weird in some ways, but let's face it, who isn't weird in some ways? Right, Russ?

The ride on old bumpity-bump Highway 56 seemed so different from inside the Jeep than on the Cushman—his late, drowned red 1952 Cushman Pacemaker.

There was Johnny Gillette's place. There was no light over the sign, so Otis couldn't read the words, but he knew they were there. He remembered what Johnny had said about being his own boss. Was he a happy man? Should Russ Tonganoxie come out here and talk to Johnny Gillette about being a mature adult male?

Otis came upon the location of Mary Beth's café. But in the dark, at first glance, it appeared to be no longer there. That couldn't be. In the shadows, he saw only the skeletal scraps of a building.

He slammed on the brakes turned the Jeep in to the small front parking area and looked around.

The place had burned down! Literally down to the ground.

There were only a few charred bricks and scarred remains of the counter and the kitchen and the chrome booth frames on what was left of the tile floor. Even the MARY BETH'S EATS sign was almost gone. He saw what seemed to be pieces of the metal backing on the ground, but the neon glass had clearly melted away, the wooden post on which it had all hung burned almost to a crisp.

Otis recalled what that man—a relative, they'd said—had threatened to Mary Beth. He had said that someday she and her café were going to burn up as if they were in hell itself. Otis, on reflex, looked down at some ashes on the tile floor. Could they be Mary Beth's? That was a ridiculous thought.

But did that crazy man carry out his threat? Did he burn this place down? Did she burn down, too? Otis couldn't get over the fact that it had been only six weeks since he was here. Six weeks plus a few days. Hard to imagine that. Six weeks plus a few days.

Soon he was back in the Jeep on his way west again.

It was unseasonably cool for an evening in early June. The night air was fresh, and the sky was clear and bright from a three-quarter moon and a sprinkling of stars, most of which he had always been able to identify. From a moving Jeep, it was impossible to do much more than see and appreciate the moon that was out there in front of him—probably right over Pagosa Springs, Colorado, at this moment.

There was very little man-made lighting. No streetlights, and no electric signs from service stations or the few businesses that now were closed. There were even fewer cars and other vehicles. Old U.S. 56 appeared even more deserted and ignored and forgotten at night than in the daylight. The sight of a disintegrated Mary Beth's—another addition to Kansas's ghost places—had made it seem even more deserted, ignored, forgotten: dead and sad.

Someday, if he ever came back this way, he would try to find out what had happened to Mary Beth and her café.

But now it was onward, Buck.

He needed money so he could pick up some clothes and other basics. What about a toothbrush and a razor and some shaving cream? Those kind of runaway decisions could wait. He was determined not to stop for anything until he was beyond the Chanute River Bridge. That was important to him for reasons that probably made no sense, reasons that had to do with a feeling of really being gone, of escape. Past the bridge, he would be free.

But he definitely needed money. He had his MasterCard, which had been left—thank God!—with his now-dried-out driver's license on a shelf in his closet with his clothes. But where was he going to find an ATM around here?

He had an inspired Buck-like thought. There was one location in the vicinity where there was a very good chance money was available.

There was no traffic coming toward him, so he carefully U-turned the Jeep back toward the east, toward Church Key Charlie Blue's.

It seemed like only a flash of time before he was there once more. He again slowed the Jeep and, as he arrived at the lip of the driveway, switched off the motor and the headlights.

The TV was still flickering inside.

Otis sat absolutely still in the darkness. He wanted to make sure he had not been heard, that Charlie had not been roused to come out the door and see what might be going on in his driveway.

After what seemed to be at least two or three minutes, Otis decided that Charlie had not been disturbed.

He stepped out of the Jeep and walked as quietly as he

could—the slippers helped—to the window. The panes on top had not been replaced; they were covered over from the inside with what appeared to be plastic bags. Some new glass was on the other panes.

Did you use some of my money to have the panes replaced, Charlie, you shithead?

Otis peeked inside. Just as he had hoped and expected, Charlie was in his chair in front of the television, fast asleep.

Otis may have imagined it, but he thought he could hear snoring over the sound of the television. He did not recognize the sounds enough to know what program Charlie had been watching when he fell asleep. Whatever it was, it seemed to involve several vehicles in a frantic chase of some kind, because there were a lot of tires squealing, horns honking, and shots being fired.

There was enough moonlight to help Otis find his way around to the rear. Charlie had said the back door was never locked.

Otis grabbed the knob on the first door he came to and opened it slowly, carefully, quietly. Through the opening, he saw Charlie and the television. The sweet smell of fudge came right at Otis. So did the sounds of snoring and the car chase, which seemed to still be in full throttle.

There, by the side of the chair, was the Cowboys helmet. Charlie had clearly come directly from the factory to the chair in front of the television: A pair of soiled latex gloves was lying there with the helmet.

Here I am, Charlie. Remember me? I was here the first time as Oat-tus. I'm back as Buh-uhk.

Otis stepped over some empty Great America beer bottles and empty paper plates and bags and other things. He extended every step into a giant step and paused between each to make sure he had not disturbed the sleeping, thieving giant shithead in the chair before him.

Charlie's right arm was hanging over the side of the chair, almost down to the floor where the helmet was. His fingers, nearly the size of some people's wrists, were within inches of the helmet, which was lying inside up—*money* side up.

Assuming the money was still there. What if Charlie had spent it or used it to pay off his debts?

There's no turning back now, Buck.

Two more steps and he was there. Otis leaned down and picked up the helmet, being careful to bring it away and up so as not to touch Charlie's dangling hand or arm.

Otis was only two or so feet from Charlie. The force of the man's breathing was enormous. The television, still spewing out the sounds of cars and shots, seemed minor and small and insignificant compared to the presence of this huge human being.

The money was in the webbing. Both stacks of Otis's bills as well as more. That must be some of the money Charlie made from his fudge. There was several hundred dollars in addition to the four thou. Charlie had yet to make enough to buy his freedom.

Sorry, Charlie. Wasn't that a line from an old television commercial? Yeah, yeah. For a brand of tuna fish.

Otis removed the money—his and Charlie's—from the helmet and stuck it all in his pants pockets.

Consider your money interest on mine, *Charlie.*

Nope. No way could Buck do that. That made him a thief, too, and no better than this thieving, sleeping, snoring shithead.

Otis slipped Charlie's part of the money back out of the pants pockets and returned it to its place inside the helmet webbing. He was leaning over to put the helmet back on the floor when a close-up of the dirty latex gloves gave him an idea—a deliciously evil idea. Didn't the Lone Ranger and the others—Red Ryder, too, no doubt—leave calling cards behind?

Otis picked up one of the gloves and folded down the two pairs of outside fingers, leaving only the middle finger straight and pointed upward. He carefully placed the glove that way up in the webbing where the two stacks of his money had just been.

Goodbye and up yours, Charlie.

Otis thought of Church Key's fabulous fudge. He could smell it, and then he could taste it. Could there possibly be an un-bought bag, even a piece or two, lying around next door? Why not slip over there and see . . . Forget it. It was time to get the hell out of here.

When Otis glanced at the television, he was amazed that the car chase was still going on. Maybe it was a program devoted exclusively to car chases? Could there be such a thing? Could there be a television program called *Great Car Chases of Police History*?

Within a few minutes, Otis was back outside in the Jeep, on his way west once again.

Now he really was Buh-uhk.

HE ADHERED TO the fifty-five-mile-an-hour speed limit. The late Deputy Canton must have a successor, and there was a chance he or she was out there somewhere, looking for lawbreak-ers along old U.S 56. Being stopped for speeding might end it all again.

But it seemed like a flash that he was back down the road, past Johnny Gillette's and Mary Beth's, where he had been when he turned around to take care of his money needs at Charlie's.

Soon came Marionville, the town of brick streets and Galva Air Force Base and T and Iola Caldwell.

Was Iola still alive? It had been six weeks. If she had died, what kind of funeral had T organized for his mother? Did that son of a bitch of a father come from California to the service? Did Iola have insurance? What kind of policy and for how much? What was T going to do about the house? About his life?

Otis decided he had to have the answers to those and many other questions about the Caldwells. Also, he wanted to tell T how much he'd appreciated the young man's coming by the hospital and how sorry he was that he couldn't respond and they wouldn't let T in the hospital room. T might also get a kick out of hearing what Otis had just done to a thieving old football player named Church Key Charlie Blue.

Otis swung the Jeep off the highway, and within a few minutes, there was the Caldwells' house. There was a for-sale sign in the front yard, which needed mowing.

"Iola died three weeks ago," said Grace, the old woman in the blue housecoat who lived next door. She acted as if she might remember Otis from when he was there with the Cushman, but he wasn't sure. "The funeral was beautiful and sweet," she said.

Otis asked about T. Had he gone back to school?

"No, I don't think so. He packed up most everything he had and took off in his pickup. He said he had to go but wouldn't say where. It didn't sound to me like it was back to Central State he had in mind."

No, it wasn't back to school in Kansas he had in mind. He was one of those who was meant to go.

Someday, somewhere, Otis would resume some kind of relationship with T Caldwell. When? Why? Who knew? But Otis had a good feeling about it.

Then he was back on Highway 56, with Dearing coming into sight. Here now was the Best Western on the right, where he'd had that lovely wet imagined sexual encounter with Sharon.

Sharon. Who in the hell is she, really? Is she a nurse? Is she even a real person? Is it possible that I completely hallucinated her? She was not really there on the creek bank reading the Beschloss book? She didn't really take a ride up there behind me on the Cushman?

And she didn't really yank off my Chiefs helmet and look horrified at what she saw?

It was right about here that Deputy Canton stopped me. That poor man. Tries to do a good turn and dies for his effort. Someday I will look up his family and personally thank them for what he did. He saved my life. What would he have done with me if he had caught up before I fell into the river? Arrest me? On what charge? Running away from home on my own motor scooter with my own money is not a crime.

There was that first sign for the detour.

BRIDGE CLOSED AHEAD 1 MILE—FOLLOW DETOUR SIGNS. The words were painted with reflecting paint.

There were the other signs, bigger and more hysterical.

DANGER AHEAD. ALL VEHICLES MUST TURN LEFT.

The barricade of orange barrels and boards.

This time Otis did as he was told. He turned left.

Within a few minutes, it was all a few miles and thoughts behind him. What now? What new and different adventures awaited him on this second runaway? He'd already had a most satisfying one, getting his money back.

Up ahead he saw the lights of the interstate. Off to the northwest, just south of the entrance ramp, were even more lights— a small strip mall.

Otis was struck with how different these worlds of the interstate and Highway 56 were, despite running parallel to each other, only a few miles apart. They could have easily passed as highways in two very different countries.

He looked at his wristwatch. It was nine-forty-five. Nine-forty-five? Nine-forty-five! He had driven from Russ Tonganoxie's house to here in under an hour, even with the Marionville stop-off and the delay at Charlie's fudge factory.

It had been a journey of over two days the first time.

He turned off at the shopping center. He figured he might as well pick up a pair of cheap sneakers, if nothing else. Continuing to go around in slippers was not a smart thing to do.

There was a sign for a SunflowerMart, a chain of convenience-plus stores that were all over Kansas. He parked right next to the one-story building. No other cars were around; few of the other stores in the center appeared to be open. Maybe the drugstore and the Safeway over to the left were open. And the video store. Video stores always seemed to be open.

The SunflowerMart had a bin of cheap canvas shoes, and Otis found a pair of blue and white ones that were his size—nine. He also picked up a toothbrush and a safety razor.

Back in the Jeep a few seconds later, he stuck the key in the ignition.

"Mistah . . . hel—wo."

It was a thin, weak female voice behind his right ear.

He lurched forward, then turned around. Stunned, afraid.

There in the backseat, under two feet away, sat a young woman. There was enough light from the SunflowerMart for him to see her fairly well. She was shaking and crying. She was tiny, bony, messy—hurt. Her face was bruised, and there was blood on her left cheek and all over her lower lip, which was twice as big as it ought to be.

She held something with her hands tight against her chest. It was wrapped in a light blue blanket.

"What are you doing in here?" Otis asked. He tried to ask it gently, but it came out harshly, loudly. He was still recovering from the fear that her voice had shot through him.

From the blanket came the piercing cry of a baby. The woman had a baby in her arms.

"I can hard-wy talk," she said. "Please take me away—fas. Fas, fas. Pease."

"What happened to you?"

"My ex-husbund. Drunk. Come to take baby. Hit me, hit me, and then pass out. I run here. Our house over behind Safeway."

Otis couldn't tell if she was leaving out words as a matter of intellect or dialect or her injured mouth. Whatever, it came out as a form of pidgin English. Her skin was dark. She might be Hispanic or Iranian.

"How old are you?" he asked.

"Two-two . . . twennie-two."

It was hard to hear the answer over the screaming of the baby. *But why am I asking her questions like that at a time like this?*

Onward, Buck!

He started the Jeep and burned rubber out of the parking lot and back onto the access road north toward the interstate.

Annabel, when she was a baby, could always be put to sleep by the rhythm of a car ride.

Oh, Annabel. Someday I will be back to be your father. Your func-tioning father. I promise—I hope.

Riding in a car didn't work on this baby. This one, this little twenty-two-year-old beaten-up woman's baby, kept crying. It seemed to be getting louder the more he gunned the Jeep.

"He upset," said the woman as Otis drove onto the interstate. "He like me sing before he sleep. Can't do now. Mouth hurt too much."

"Do you want to go back to the shopping center and get something from the drugstore? Or go to a doctor or a hospital?"

"No! He'll be after me."

Otis couldn't see her very well in the rearview mirror. But he didn't have to see or hear to know what the answer to his question would be.

"What if *I* tried to sing something?" he asked. As if to audition, he softly sang in a radio jingles tune:

"If I loved Jill in Jeff City,
And her life made her hurt and sad,
I'd help her out of her Missouri."

"That good. Yeah, yeh. Pease. He used to hearing my voice, but maybe anybody's work. His daddy never sing."

Otis Rolodexed mentally through the Johnny Mercer songs he knew. It didn't take long to get to the one he thought might do the trick. It was a later song than those he sang in high school, but he had paid attention when it became popular in the 1960s. He knew the words that Mercer had written for Henry Mancini's music and for Audrey Hepburn. He had never sung them out loud before.

Now he sang them softly, Mercerly, for the first time to the crying baby boy in the backseat:

"Moon River,
Wider than a mile,
I'm crossin' you in style
Someday."

The baby was still crying, but it seemed to Otis that the ferocity had diminished. The kid was listening.

Listen to this, little boy blue:

"Old dream maker,
You heartbreaker,

Wherever you're goin'
I'm goin' your way."

The baby was only whimpering now. Otis wished the kid could understand the words. Maybe he could.

"Two drifters,
Off to see the world,
There's such a lot of world
To see."

Listen, kid. Listen to this:

"We're after the same
Rainbow's end
Waitin' 'round the bend,
My huckleberry friend,
Moon River
And me."

There was silence in the backseat. The only sounds now were the purring of the Jeep's motor and the whining of its tires on the smooth roadway of the interstate.

"He sleep," said the young woman in a whisper. "I lay him on seat." She had moved her head up to Otis's right ear. "You sing great, mis-tah. My baby love it, I could tell. You should make CD."

"Thank you," Otis said.

"Where we go?" she asked.

"I don't know," Otis replied.

"Okay for me," said the woman. "You seem like good and nice man. Bad man no sing like you. I so tired."

She sat back down against the seat, and soon, in the occasional flashes of car lights through the rearview mirror, Otis saw that she, like her little boy blue, was sound asleep.

After a while he pulled in to a Holiday Inn Express and used his MasterCard to buy two nights for the girl and her baby. He escorted them to their room, handed the little mother a fistful of cash—all but a few hundred of his four-plus thousand dollars.

"You really are good and nice man, mistah," said the girl.

Otis hoped she had it right.

Soon he was back out on the interstate, heading west.

He thought about finding a store where he could buy another BB gun. And hey, there had to be a sporting goods store up the road that sold football helmets. One of the antiques stores in Lehigh City, fifty miles or so ahead, might even have a cast-iron fire engine. What about another Cushman?

Or maybe not.

Otis wondered if Archimedes felt as good as this when he shouted "Eureka!"

Or on the night before *his* sixtieth birthday.

This is JIM LEHRER's seventeenth novel. He is also the author of two memoirs and three plays and is the executive editor and anchor of *The NewsHour with Jim Lehrer* on PBS. He and his novelist wife, Kate, have three daughters.

ABOUT THE TYPE

This book was set in Garamond No. 3, a variation of the classic Garamond typeface originally designed by the Parisian type cutter Claude Garamond (1480–1561).

Claude Garamond's distinguished romans and italics first appeared in *Opera Ciceronis* in 1543–44. The Garamond types are clear, open, and elegant.